"I have no interest in you as a man."

Tucker pushed his hat back and planted his hands on his hips. "Liar, I watched you watch me walk over. Your eyes were eating me up like I was a big stick of candy."

Cassie gasped. *Had she been so obvious?* "I did not."

"And your lips told a different story just a minute ago. You liked kissing me...until your brain got in the way."

Why did he have to be so perceptive? "All right, I liked it. But that doesn't mean I want to do it again."

"Liar," he said softly.

"I just want to make it clear on the front end that this trip is strictly business. No kissing, no touching, no suggestive comments."

Tucker stared at her so long and so hard Cassie's palms began to sweat. "Do you agree, Mr. Reeves?"

"Hell, no."

Dear Reader,

Looking for sensational summer reads? All year we've been celebrating Silhouette's 20th Anniversary with special titles, and this month's selections are just the warm, romantic tales you've been seeking!

Bestselling author Stella Bagwell continues the newest Romance promotion, AN OLDER MAN. *Falling for Grace* hadn't been his intention, particularly when his younger, *pregnant* neighbor was carrying his nephew's baby! Judy Christenberry's THE CIRCLE K SISTERS miniseries comes back to Romance this month, when sister Melissa enlists the temporary services of *The Borrowed Groom.* Moyra Tarling's *Denim & Diamond* pairs a rough-hewn single dad with the expectant woman he'd once desired beyond reason...but let get away.

Valerie Parv unveils her romantic royalty series THE CARRAMER CROWN. When a woman literally washes ashore at the feet of the prince, she becomes companion to *The Monarch's Son*...but will she ever become the monarch's wife? Julianna Morris's BRIDAL FEVER! persists when *Jodie's Mail-Order Man* discovers her heart's desire: the *brother* of her mail-order groom! And Martha Shields's *Lassoed!* is the perfect Opposites Attract story this summer. The sparks between a rough-and-tumble rodeo champ and the refined beauty sent to photograph him jump off every page!

In future months, look for STORKVILLE, USA, our newest continuity series. And don't miss the charming miniseries THE CHANDLERS REQUEST... from *New York Times* bestselling author Kasey Michaels.

Happy reading!

Mary-Theresa Hussey

Mary-Theresa Hussey
Senior Editor

Please address questions and book requests to:
Silhouette Reader Service
U.S.: 3010 Walden Ave., P.O. Box 1325, Buffalo, NY 14269
Canadian: P.O. Box 609, Fort Erie, Ont. L2A 5X3

Lassoed!

MARTHA SHIELDS

Silhouette

ROMANCE™

Published by Silhouette Books

America's Publisher of Contemporary Romance

To Amelia, my soul sister.
Tucker has always been for you.

Special thanks to Beverly Rucker of Brasher-Rucker Photography in Memphis for photographic information.

SILHOUETTE BOOKS

ISBN 0-373-19461-7

LASSOED!

Copyright © 2000 by Martha Shields

Visit Silhouette at www.eHarlequin.com

Printed in U.S.A.

Books by Martha Shields

Silhouette Romance

Home Is Where Hank Is #1287
And Cowboy Makes Three #1317
The Million-Dollar Cowboy #1346
Husband Found #1377
The Princess and the Cowboy #1403
Lassoed! #1461

*Cowboys to the Rescue

MARTHA SHIELDS

grew up telling stories to her sister to pass time on the long drives to their grandparents' house. Since she's never been able to stop dreaming up characters, she's thrilled to share her stories with a wider audience. Martha lives in Memphis, Tennessee, with her husband, teenage daughter and a Cairn "terror" who can't believe he's not in Kansas anymore. Martha has a master's degree in journalism and works at a local university.

You can keep up with Martha's new releases via her Web site, which can be reached through the author page at www.eHarlequin.com.

IT'S OUR 20th ANNIVERSARY!
We'll be celebrating all year,
Continuing with these fabulous titles,
On sale in July 2000.

Intimate Moments

#1015 Egan Cassidy's Kid
Beverly Barton

#1016 Mission: Irresistible
Sharon Sala

#1017 The Once and Future Father
Marie Ferrarella

#1018 Imminent Danger
Carla Cassidy

#1019 The Detective's Undoing
Jill Shalvis

#1020 Who's Been Sleeping in Her Bed?
Pamela Dalton

Special Edition

#1333 The Pint-Sized Secret
Sherryl Woods

#1334 Man of Passion
Lindsay McKenna

#1335 Whose Baby Is This?
Patricia Thayer

#1336 Married to a Stranger
Allison Leigh

#1337 Doctor and the Debutante
Pat Warren

#1338 Maternal Instincts
Beth Henderson

Desire

#1303 Bachelor Doctor
Barbara Boswell

#1304 Midnight Fantasy
Ann Major

#1305 Wife for Hire
Amy J. Fetzer

#1306 Ride a Wild Heart
Peggy Moreland

#1307 Blood Brothers
Anne McAllister & Lucy Gordon

#1308 Cowboy for Keeps
Kristi Gold

Romance

#1456 Falling for Grace
Stella Bagwell

#1457 The Borrowed Groom
Judy Christenberry

#1458 Denim & Diamond
Moyra Tarling

#1459 The Monarch's Son
Valerie Parv

#1460 Jodie's Mail-Order Man
Julianna Morris

#1461 Lassoed!
Martha Shields

Chapter One

So many cowboys. So little—

Cassie Burch stopped dead, her name-brand athletic shoes kicking up dust from the dirt floor of the Silver Spurs arena.

Where had that thought come from?

As if she'd make a move even if she didn't have to catch an evening flight out of Orlando. She was not interested in males of any kind, much less these macho creatures who had not stopped hitting on her or helping her since she'd walked into the area behind the chutes.

She hadn't so much as picked up a dropped lens cover. Before she could reach for it, a calloused, strong-fingered cowboy hand had already retrieved it, dusted it off and offered it to her.

She hadn't said, "Thank you" so many times since last year when she'd won her last commercial photography award.

Cassie gave a mental snort and dragged her eyes away from the row of jeans'-clad cowboy bottoms perched like round, indigo birds atop the fence curving away from the rough stock chutes. Squinting against the late afternoon sun she was trying to put behind her, she continued along the path.

Halfway between the cowboys and the spectators, she reached up to haul herself to the top rail. She hadn't even flexed her biceps, however, when a pair of strong hands wrapped around her waist.

"Let me help you, ma'am," said a deep cowboy twang.

Before she could blink, she'd been shoved high enough to easily lift a leg over the fence. She caught her balance, then sent a dry smile down to the square-jawed face beaming up at her. "Thank you."

He tipped his hat. "My pleasure, ma'am."

Cassie dragged her legs over the rail and settled on the top plank. She'd never been "ma'amed" so much in her life. You'd think she was eighty instead of twenty-eight.

With a defeated sigh, she checked the state of the four cameras hanging around her neck in anticipation of the bull riding—the last event of this Kissimmee, Florida, rodeo.

Satisfied everything was in order, she allowed her gaze to drift back to the men behind the chutes. Some worked feverishly, helping the men preparing to ride. Some stood around talking. They all wore what seemed to be the cowboy uniform—Wrangler blue jeans, cowboy boots and hat, and a long-sleeved shirt with snaps instead of buttons.

"Slap your eyes on chute number three, ladies and gentlemen!" the rodeo announcer bid the spectators.

A murmur went through the crowd.

Lifting a camera, Cassie focused on the chute halfway across the arena that sported a small number three and a large ad for a local truck dealer.

The announcer continued. "Three-time World Bull Riding Champion Tucker Reeves from Kiowa, Colorado, is up first in the bull riding."

This cowboy was evidently a popular one. Cassie could feel the crowd's excitement—like electricity in the air. She leaned forward and craned to the left to see him settle on the bull. She recognized a man she'd photographed earlier behind the chutes. Rugged, handsome. The quintessential cowboy.

"He's drawn Crazy Eight! Folks, this bull has only been ridden one time this season. But Tucker has won four national championships for bull riding, so if anyone can do it, he's the man."

Four national championships. Good. He would probably stay on long enough for her to get some decent shots. She'd discovered during the bronc riding that eight seconds wasn't very long.

The helpers backed away, lining up on the deck behind the chute. Through her telephoto lens, Cassie saw the rider firmly seat his hat on his head and scoot forward until he practically sat on the hand that held the bull rope.

The crowd hushed, holding its collective breath, watching for the cowboy's signal.

He glanced at someone standing above him, allowing Cassie to glimpse his face. As she snapped a few frames, she saw he was indeed the same man she'd noticed earlier as she shot a group of cowboys standing behind the chutes "jawin'," as one had put it.

He was the kind of man who would stand out in any crowd—tall, broad-shouldered, with a jaw hewn out of granite.

The cowboy gave a slight nod. Cheers erupted as the gate swung open and an ugly, mottled-brown bull with widespread horns flung himself into the arena. With a snort of fury, Crazy Eight spun to the left, then kicked high in the air.

Click-whirrrr-click-whirrrr-click-whirrrr-click-whirrrr.

Cassie could barely hear the automatic shutter above the roar of the crowd. She was certain her camera caught the massive animal with his heels pointed straight at the sky.

The bull hit the dirt and began spinning to the right.

"Erica, you're going to love this," Cassie muttered.

The rider stayed glued to the bull's immense back, his attention riveted at some point between the horns. He made it look easy, like a Sunday afternoon ride in the park, even though he was whiplashed with every turn. He was taller than the other bull riders, his spurs raking the belly of the monster.

With each jump, the whirling dervish came closer to Cassie's perch.

She dropped her camera on its strap and felt blindly at her waist for the one with the fifty millimeter lens. She whipped it up, focusing and shooting without sparing a thought.

More spins. More kicks. More clicks and whirrs.

The timer buzzed loudly and the cowboy bailed out in mid-kick. He flew through the air and landed hard on his feet just fifteen yards in front of her. He struggled for balance and glanced behind him.

Cassie gasped. The bull pawed the dirt, head down, then charged at him.

The cowboy sprinted for safety. Even with his long strides, he couldn't outrun the bull.

Cassie's mouth went dry as the cowboy zigged, but she kept her lens focused and her finger on the shutter button.

He headed straight for her, his hat flying off his head.

She blessed her luck.

As he came closer, she leaned to the right to keep the bull in the frame.

She realized her mistake too late. Just as she leaned, the cowboy leaped for the fence.

Tucker cussed when his face missed smashing into the camera by a hairbreadth. He felt the photographer falling back and grabbed instinctively.

Surprised to feel a woman's figure, he twisted as his hips cleared the top plank and they sailed back through the air. He caught a whiff of roses, then a red rope of hair slapped him across the face as her head whipped around.

He glimpsed a piquant face with huge green eyes before a sudden flash blinded him. Then he hit the hard-packed dirt.

As the air was driven from his lungs, an image popped into his head—the red-haired, green-eyed angel who'd shone from atop the Christmas tree when he was a young boy.

A faint smile curved across his lips. He'd heard that your life flashed before your eyes when you were dying.

Then the world turned black.

Cassie's face thudded into a hard chest. She lay stunned, breathing a mixture of man, dirt and bull, her mind trying to comprehend what had just happened.

When she finally realized that none of her bones were broken, she groaned and tried to sit up, but found herself trapped in a snare of straps.

Her cameras. Not only did this cowboy take the brunt of her weight, she'd gouged him on the way down.

She hurriedly worked her cameras free from her arms and neck, and his hands. Her heart pounded so loudly she couldn't hear anything else. When she finally freed herself from the tangle, she straightened and looked down.

The cowboy's eyes were closed, but she remembered a flash of neon blue before he hit the ground. His face was strong with a square jaw and a nose that looked as if it had been broken more than once. Permanent dimples bracketed each side of his full lips, which curved softly. His dark hair was short and spiky, almost begging a woman's hands to run through the thick strands.

There was only one problem... He wasn't moving.

She leaned over and patted his face hesitantly. "Mr. Reeves? Tucker Reeves? Wake up."

He didn't respond.

She slapped his face harder. "Wake up. Please! I've shot people, but never killed them."

No response to the old photography joke.

"Help!" A glance toward the chutes told Cassie help was almost there. Cowboys of all shapes and sizes were running their way. "Hurry!"

The first cowboy there took her elbow. "Are you all right?"

"I'm fine." She shrugged him off. "But I think he's dead."

An older cowboy took her arm more gently and urged her

up. She resisted until he explained, "We need to let him breathe."

Only then did Cassie realize she still straddled the cowboy's chest. Mortified at adding insult to injury, she allowed the older man to help her stand.

"Oooohhh."

"He's waking up," said a cowboy kneeling next to the injured man.

"He's alive!" Relief made Cassie's knees buckle. She sank down on his other side.

She reached for the large, tanned hand lying limply across his chest. But as she touched his warm skin, she realized she'd intended to hold it against her pounding heart. Luckily, twenty-eight years of practice at holding her emotions in check saved her.

Instead of mooning over his hand like a silly schoolgirl, she slapped it repeatedly. "Wake up, Mr. Reeves. Please."

His eyes fluttered open and focused on her. Caught by intense blue surrounded by a tanned face and dark brown hair, she couldn't look away until a man above her cleared his throat.

"Ma'am? If you'd kindly move outta the way so's we can get at Tucker, we'd be obliged."

Tucker was lucid enough to understand what Rodeo Director Sam Weston was saying. He also knew how important it was to keep this angel by his side, though the waves of pain pounding in his brain kept him from knowing exactly why. He only knew that he'd lost his angel once, and he'd be damned before he lost her again.

He immediately seized the angel's hand to prevent her from rising. He shook his head slightly but instead of clearing, his brain rattled painfully around his skull. "Oooohh-hhh."

"Don't go moving around, Tuck, till we check you out."

Since his scope of focus was limited, Tucker ignored the man kneeling next to his angel and the men on his left who were preparing a stretcher. Instead, he concentrated on beautiful green eyes. "Who are you?"

She tried to pull her hand from his, but he held tight.

After glancing at the men hovering above, she said, "Cassie. Please. You need to let them help you."

His groggy mind mixed the real image with memory. "Cassie Angel."

"Angel?" She chuckled nervously. "You *are* out of it."

"No. I want—"

"Tucker, we need to get you checked out."

"Go away, Sam." Tucker focused on Cassie. "Come closer."

Her eyes narrowed in confusion, but she leaned down.

"Closer."

She came within inches of his face. Tucker released her hand, caught the back of her neck and pulled her mouth the rest of the way down. As her lips touched his, he ignored her gasp and the hoots of the cowboys around them.

Her lips were stiff with surprise, but he held on until angel lips melted against his.

"You taste like heaven," he whispered when he finally released her.

"Miss?" Sam Weston cleared his throat. "You need to move out of the way. We've got to get him on the stretcher."

"Stretcher, hell. I'm all right." Tucker tried to sit up but four pairs of strong hands held him down. Pain and nausea swept through him, so he couldn't fight them.

Sam nudged Cassie aside. "You know the rules at this arena, Tucker. You get knocked out, you get checked out. At the hospital."

"Hell, Weston, you're just trying to cover your butt." Tucker tried to snarl but obviously wasn't successful because Sam didn't seem intimidated.

"You got that right," the rodeo director said. "But you entered the rodeo under my rules. Now shut up and let us get you on the stretcher."

Tucker caught Cassie's hand when she straightened. "I'll be back in a couple of hours. Wait for me."

He tried to cling to her but four husky cowboys shouldered her aside, and he didn't have the strength to fight them.

When her hand slipped from his, he felt as though he'd just lost his best horse.

"Always did hate steer wrestlers," he muttered to the men bending down.

"We'll remember that next time you want to share a plane to Amarillo," said one.

"Or Cheyenne," said another.

"Or anywheres," agreed a third.

"I'm okay," Tucker growled as they lifted him onto the stretcher. "Damn it, boys, I just found my Christmas angel. I can't go to a hospital."

"Christmas ain't for another ten months, Tuck."

"That you, Clay?" Clay Hicks was his traveling partner, but Tucker couldn't see anything through the damn chambray shirts carrying him away. "Don't let her out of your sight, Clay!"

"Who, Tuck?"

"Cassie Angel."

"Uh, sure, Tuck. Anything you say."

Cassie hesitated inside the waiting area at the emergency room and glanced around at the Saturday night chaos. She shouldn't have come. Her plane for New York left in less than two hours.

But she couldn't not come. She had to know if Tucker Reeves was going to be okay.

She'd tried to convince herself that her feelings were simple human concern, but the feel of his lips on hers popped into her mind every time, mocking her attempts to explain this need with logic.

There was no logic in being here. She simply had to come. Why did she need to explain herself...to herself?

Spotting a black cowboy hat on a man seated across the room, Cassie approached the cowboy and tapped him on the shoulder. "Clay Hicks?"

He turned around and squinted up at her. "Yep? Who's askin'?"

"I'm Cassie Burch. Sam told me to ask for you. Have you heard how—"

"Cassie?"

"Yes."

"From the arena?"

"Well…yes. I just wanted to—"

"Hellfire. It's about time." The cowboy hopped up from his seat, took Cassie's arm and dragged her toward the desk.

She tried to pull her arm from his iron grip. "What are you doing?"

"Tucker's been asking for you for the last hour." He hauled her in front of the registration desk. "This here's Cassie Angel."

"Thank God," breathed an obviously relieved nurse.

She jumped out of her chair and ushered Cassie through a set of swinging doors. "This cowboy's been throwing fits at every nurse passing by. In between, he's been singing at the top of his lungs—Christmas carols, hymns about angels, songs about you, about someone named Morey that we finally figured out was a dog. And let me tell you, this cowboy's no Gene Autry. His voice is about to split our eardrums."

As Cassie was rushed down a short hallway lined with empty gurneys, a drunken, twangy voice singing an off-key version of "White Christmas" echoed off the industrial-tile walls.

Two seconds later, she was thrust into a brightly lit examining room.

The singing stopped abruptly.

"Your Cassie Angel's here," the nurse announced before deserting her.

"S'about time." The prone figure on the table, clad only in

jeans and socks, slowly lifted to one elbow. The bright blue eyes Cassie hadn't been able to forget were dull with pain.

"Cassie Angel," he breathed.

She cleared her throat. "Well, I'm Cassie...but I'm no angel."

One dark brow rose. "Aren't you?"

"No."

He smiled softly. "Come closer."

"Uh-uh." She shook her head, more to shake off the seductive tones than to emphasize her refusal. "That won't work twice."

He gave her a lopsided grin. "Too bad."

Her heart beat a sharp staccato, and Cassie took enough grudging steps to cover half the distance to the table. "How are you?"

"I've been better," he said with a shrug.

Her eyes cut to his shirt hanging on a hook. There was blood on the collar. "Have you seen a doctor?"

"Just long enough for him to order X rays."

"So you don't know anything yet."

He shook his head, then grimaced. "The only thing I know is that I'm glad you're finally here."

"But..." She swallowed hard. "Why on earth would you think I'd come? I shouldn't have. My plane leaves in less than two hours."

"You're my angel," he said as if that explained everything.

"Mr. Reeves—"

"Tucker."

"*Mr. Reeves,* I'm not now and never will be anybody's angel."

With another painful wince, he lay back down.

She took a step closer. "Are you all right?"

He held out his hand. "Come closer, Angel."

She couldn't. She shouldn't. She had a plane to catch.

"Please." He sighed and closed his eyes.

His pain was her fault. If he would be comforted by holding

her hand for a few minutes...well, didn't she owe him that much?

Taking an uneven breath, she stepped forward and slipped her hand into his. He immediately laced their fingers, locking her in place. Palm to palm, his heat warmed more than her hand.

Cassie wasn't stupid. She recognized the heat for what it was—physical attraction. She'd been attracted to several men before and had been able to resist them. So why did she feel...almost scared...this time?

Okay, maybe her attraction to the man was a little stronger than she'd felt in the past, but there was no reason to be frightened. If nothing else, there wasn't time to succumb. She'd be on a plane in two hours and would never see this cowboy again.

Cassie frowned. That thought should make her happy. It shouldn't make her want to howl like a lonesome puppy the first night away from his mother and littermates.

She pulled her hand from his.

Tucker opened his eyes. "Where are you going?"

"I have to catch a plane."

"You can't leave." He reached for her hand.

"Don't be ridiculous. I have to. My plane leaves in—" she eluded his hand by glancing at her watch "—an hour and forty-two minutes."

"Take a later plane." He sat up with a grimace. "Like next week. Or next year."

"Very funny." She backed toward the door. "Listen, I only came to make sure you're all right. It's my fault you're hurt, after all."

"How do you figure that?" He slipped off the table.

"Well, if I hadn't been on that fence, in the way, you'd probably have cleared it without being injured. But you look fine now, so I'll be going." Feeling the door against her back, she turned and grabbed the knob.

But suddenly he was there. His stiff, bare arm kept her from opening it. "You can't go. Not yet."

She felt him looming over her. His warmth pressed against her back, threatening to overwhelm her senses. If she didn't get out of here—now—she was going to…well, she didn't know what she would do. She only knew that it would feel like heaven now, and make her feel like hell later. "I have to."

"What about us?" With a finger on her chin, he made her look at him.

"What 'us'? There is no 'us.' We just met. You'll forget about me by tomorrow."

"Like hell I will. And what does just meeting have to do with anything? Are you trying to tell me you're not attracted to me? That at this very moment, you can't feel the earth move? You don't hear choirs of angels?"

"Yes. No." She cleared her throat. "I'm not attracted to you, okay? If you feel, see or hear any of that, it's because of your brain injury."

"Save your breath, Angel." His head lowered by minute degrees. "You want me. I could feel it when we kissed at the arena. I can see it in your eyes now."

"No," she whispered, mesmerized by his mouth coming closer.

"Hell, I can smell it on you." He sniffed deeply. "Like the world's most expensive, most intoxicating perfume."

His lips were a hairbreadth from hers when the door shoved against her. The only thing that kept Cassie from being hit was Tucker's quick reflexes.

"What the—?" came a male voice from the other side. "Mr. Reeves?"

"It must be your doctor." The spell was broken. Cassie once again felt like howling, but she didn't know whether it was relief, anger or frustration. "I have to go."

He grabbed her arm. "No."

The doctor carefully pushed the door open and peered in with a raised eyebrow. "Mr. Reeves?"

"Yeah, that's me," Tucker growled. He'd been waiting over an hour for the doctor. Why couldn't the stupid man have waited ten more minutes?

The doctor stepped into the room. "Please sit down, Mr. Reeves."

"I was just leaving." Cassie tried to pull her arm from Tucker's grip.

Tucker wasn't about to let go. "Stay. I'll be out of here in—"

"No," she whispered harshly. "I can't. My plane leaves in an hour and a half, and I still have to drive to Orlando."

"Then give me your phone number," Tucker insisted.

The doctor cleared his throat. "Mr. Reeves?"

"Let go of me, Tucker," Cassie said firmly. "I have to leave."

"But—"

"Now."

His head pounding with frustration, Tucker looked between Cassie and the doctor, who watched them with narrowed eyes.

"I don't need this, Tucker."

Cassie's words made him instantly release her arm. She scurried around the doctor and out the door.

I don't need this.

Her words made twenty-seven years fall away. He was seven years old, running downstairs on the first Christmas morning after his parents died. Running to see the angel shining from the top of the Christmas tree. Just as he caught sight of her, an older foster brother tripped him.

The ten-year-old stood over him and sneered, "Who needs you?"

How many times after that had he seen other shining angels, only to be tripped again—one way or another? He didn't know at what point he'd stopped looking for angels, but by the time he ran away from the Texas foster care system at sixteen, he'd learned the lesson well.

Who needs you?

It was the theme of his life.

But even those hard-won lessons couldn't stop him from stepping into the hall. "Cassie!"

She stopped abruptly—her hands poised to open the swinging doors.

He willed her to turn, convinced that if she left, he'd never see another angel again this side of heaven.

She hesitated a few seconds, then shook her head and pushed on through.

Frustration sliced through his brain like a thousand knives.

He didn't know her phone number or where she lived. He didn't even know her last name.

"Please sit down, Mr. Reeves," the doctor said. "We need to talk."

Tucker turned and glared at the nearly bald doctor who couldn't be much more than thirty. The man didn't look away. Finally, Tucker did. He couldn't blame the doctor for Cassie running out on him. It was his own fault for being so unlovable that not even an angel could want him.

The doctor pointed to the examining table. "Please. Sit down."

His body taut with defeat, his head throbbing, Tucker let the door close and walked over to lean against the table while the doctor settled on a rolling stool.

The doctor spent a minute looking over the chart in his hands, then looked up. "You've had a concussion, Mr. Reeves."

"I kinda figured that's what it was."

"You've had them before, haven't you?"

Tucker shrugged. "Four or five. Mostly when I was younger."

"Four or five?" the doctor exclaimed. "Hasn't anyone ever told you how dangerous they can be?"

He closed his eyes. He didn't want to think about this now. He wanted to think about how to find his Cassie Angel.

"You ever hear of Rocky Blair?" the doctor asked.

"The running back? Sure."

"You know what happened to him, don't you?"

Tucker rubbed his temples. "Can't say as I've kept up with him."

"Concussions, Mr. Reeves. He was hit in the head too many times. He's not the same man who made all those touchdowns. To put it crudely, his brains are scrambled. He's not the only one. This is a common occurrence with prize-fighters and professional football players. It's called the punch-drunk syndrome. It's caused by brain damage sustained from concussions. Impaired concentration, slow thinking, slurred speech—that's what you're looking at if you continue doing what you're doing."

Tucker's eyes narrowed. "You telling me no more rodeo?"

The doctor shrugged. "I can't tell you what to do with your life. I can tell you that if you sustain many more concussions, you won't be able to remember your name, much less how to throw a lasso."

"I ride rough stock, Doc."

The doctor's face tilted slightly. "As opposed to smooth stock?"

Tucker shook his head and immediately regretted it. "As opposed to timed events. You know, roping calves, steer wrestling, team roping. Rough stock is bulls and broncs."

"Then you'd forget which end of the bull to ride."

Tucker could barely concentrate through the pain. That, more than anything, scared the hell out of him. "How many more?"

"There's no way to know. Each concussion brings you closer. You may not feel the effects for years, but each one does more damage."

"Damn." Tucker looked away. If he quit now, he'd never

have the money to build that new bunkhouse for troubled boys. "Right now I kinda need the cash."

"I realize you've got commitments. But it's something you need to think about long and hard."

Tucker held out his hand. "Thanks for the advice."

The doctor's grip was firm. "Good luck, Mr. Reeves. Here's a prescription for some painkillers. You're going to need them."

Chapter Two

"Cassie? I'm here." Erica's words blared out of the intercom into the darkroom.

Cassie started, splashing fix across the top of the developing machine.

Was it three-thirty already?

She glanced at the wall clock dimly lit by safelights. Only two minutes after her top client said she'd be here. Where had the afternoon gone?

Her gaze dropped to the eight-by-tens hanging from clips on the line stretched above developing trays. Eighteen neon-blue eyes stared back at her.

That's where the afternoon had gone. Wasted. On a man she'd never see again...didn't want to see again. A cowboy, for goodness' sake.

"Cassie? You in there?"

Cassie placed the bottle of fix on a counter and pushed a button on the intercom, buzzing Erica into the side of her New York City loft that served as her studio. She had exactly forty-eight seconds before Erica walked through the double door system that protected her darkroom from film-ruining light.

Knowing how astute her friend and benefactor could be, Cassie snatched the photos from her old-fashioned drying rack and slid them into a folder. She'd just tucked the folder in a drawer when she heard the outer door to the darkroom open.

Seconds later, Erica knocked on the inside door. "Is it safe?"

Cassie picked up the bottle of fix and tightened the lid. "Come on in."

Erica entered with a friendly smile and plopped her date book on the nearest counter. "Hi. What are you up to?"

"I was just about to develop a couple of black-and-white rolls I took on the Disney shoot." She switched on the developing machine and tore off two paper towels to wipe up the spilled fix.

"How'd the color photos turn out?"

"They're on the light table. Turn it on and see for yourself."

Erica flicked on the light table, then bent over the first sleeve of color transparencies.

Cassie flipped on the overhead lights, then glanced at Erica. From the knees up she looked like the successful advertising account executive that she was. She wore a pink-and-black wool suit that was chic, business-like and feminine all at the same time. Her nearly black hair was swept back into a French twist today and as usual, not an eyelash was out of place.

Erica's legs, however, looked more like a hooker's than a businesswoman's, with a skirt that ended a few inches above her knees and black stiletto heels.

Erica's eyes scanned the rows of color slides, then she picked up another sleeve. "Anything that'll knock my socks off?"

Cassie chuckled. "Have you ever worn a pair of socks in your life?"

"Bite your tongue," Erica said in melodramatic tones. "That would mean I might actually lift a finger to— Hey, these weren't taken at Disney World."

Cassie knew which photos Erica was talking about. "It's a rodeo. I saw an article on it in the Orlando paper Friday morning and finished with the kids in time to do background shots for that men's fragrance you want me to shoot."

"They have cowboys in Florida?"

"Amazing, isn't it? Apparently, they're all over. I mean, you expect them in Texas or Wyoming, but Florida? Tennessee? New Jersey?"

"Well, I'll be lassoed," Erica said in a lousy imitation of a cowboy. "If there are that many rodeos, then there are millions of rodeo fans. Looks like I need to do some research of my own. Richman Fragrances may be tapping into a bigger market than I thought." She bent further over the light table. "Let's see what you've got here. These are really good, Cassie. What I can see, anyway. It's hard to tell much when the people are half an inch high. Not that your pictures aren't always good."

"Yeah, well you always wax rhapsodic over my photos."

"I can't help it. You're so good at capturing the emotions of your subjects—even if it's just an underwear ad. When are you going to admit it?"

Cassie knew her photos didn't take any special talent. They were the result of voyeurism, pure and simple. She liked to touch people—but only through the eye of her camera. She felt safe behind the lens. Invisible, almost. She could capture the way a subject felt without ever getting close to them, or letting them get close to her.

"Come over here. Who is this cowboy? Damn, I wish I could see this better."

Cassie frowned as she crossed the darkroom. She knew before looking which cowboy Erica had singled out. One glance at the tiny form at the end of Erica's hot pink fingernail verified it.

"Who is he?" Erica demanded.

"He's a bull rider...I think." She knew perfectly well Tucker Reeves was a bull rider, but she didn't want Erica to know she knew anything about him. Cassie hadn't shown interest in any man for nearly three years, and Erica was entirely too astute.

"What's his name?"

"His name? There were six events with ten or eleven contestants in each one. And you expect me to remember names?"

"I do for this cowboy."

"Erica…"

"Pardon me for forgetting you're not human. Can you blow him up for me?"

Erica's choice of words made a very vivid picture pop into Cassie's mind. "How…" She coughed to clear her throat. "How big do you want him?"

Erica chuckled softly and gave her a naughty grin. "How about life-size, in living color? And don't forget three-dimensional."

Erica's humor made Cassie relax. "Sorry. All out of three-dimensional developer. And my largest developing tray is only six feet."

"He's over six feet? You do remember him."

Cassie cursed her slip. "All right, I remember him. Who wouldn't?"

"Who wouldn't, indeed? Now, about that photo…"

Cassie's gaze fell on the drawer across the room. Should she admit she'd already made several eight-by-tens of Tucker, or should she drag out the bottles of developer and fix for color prints? With a defeated sigh, she retrieved the folder. "Here, I've already…blown him up."

Erica's carefully shaped black brow lifted. "Well, well, well. You *do* remember this cowboy, don't you?"

Cassie's shoulder lifted. "He…was a good subject."

"And just what did he *subject* you to?"

Erica looked at her so knowingly that Cassie rolled her eyes. "Nothing, Erica. I took pictures, then I got on a plane." She shoved the photos into Erica's hands. "Get the picture?"

"Oh, ho, a little darkroom humor. What's the famous saying about protesting too much?" But she let go of that bone and held a photo under the light. "Oh, my. My, my, my, my, my, yes! I can see why you remember this cowboy. He's got 'sexy' tattooed across his forehead."

Cassie glanced over Erica's shoulder. It was uncanny. As many photographs as she'd seen, she'd never seen one where the eyes followed you. But these did—like blue spotlights.

"He does, doesn't he?" she murmured.

"I'll say. What did you say his name was?"

The words leaped to her mouth without passing through her brain first. "Tucker Reeves."

Erica's head snapped up. "So, you do know it."

Cassie groaned. "You did that on purpose."

"Of course. I was getting those 'she's not telling me something' vibes."

Cassie looked away. No way was she telling Erica that she couldn't stop thinking about Tucker. "He's some big-shot cowboy from Colorado. Won the world title in bull riding several times. That's all I know. I swear."

Erica's eyes gleamed. "He's perfect, you know. He is *Lasso.*"

Cassie stared at her in horror. "No. You can't be thinking what I think you're thinking."

"Oh, yes, I can."

"You can't want him to appear in the ads for the new men's cologne. He's not a model."

"He could be. Look at him."

Cassie didn't need to. She'd stared at his picture so much she knew every whisker on his chin. "You can't be serious."

"Dead."

"Erica, he's a professional cowboy. He goes from one rodeo to another, riding bulls. He made nearly three thousand dollars for making one ride—for eight seconds of work. You think he wants to give that up to come to New York and pose for me?''

"He might if we offer him enough money."

"No, Erica. He's all wrong. You know you trust my judgment on models. I was thinking about Kirk Dodson for the..."

Erica shook her head. "Too young."

"Steve Lucas?"

"Too muscular."

"Chad Gray?"

"Too blond. No, Cassie, I want Tucker Reeves." She held up slender hands. "Hear me out. It's brilliant. He'll do more than pose. He will *be Lasso.*"

Cassie blinked. "You're talking about an endorsement contract."

"You bet I am. They're all the rage. And who better to represent a cologne called *Lasso* than a man whose life revolves around rope? He'd be instant identification for that huge market you were talking about."

As Cassie's list of arguments diminished, she began to worry. Tucker Reeves got to her on a level that hadn't been reached in...well, ever. "I...don't know if I can work with him. That's why you let me select the models for every job. I know what kind of emotion I can get out of Kirk or Steve or Chad."

Erica pointed at the picture. "You got this out of him, didn't you? That's what we want. Raw sex. That's what will sell this cologne."

"I didn't get that out of him. I took these before the rodeo started. I used a telephoto lens. He didn't even know I was taking them."

"Well, just think what you'll be able to do when you have his attention."

"Erica, I..." Cassie took a deep breath and released it slowly. "You're not going to give up, are you?"

The perfectly outlined pink lips curved upward. "You know me well."

"What if he can't or won't do it?"

"He can't be making three thousand dollars for every eight seconds of the day. How much money does he make in a year?"

Cassie lifted a shoulder. "I have no idea."

Erica nodded. "I'll do some research so we'll know just how much to offer before you call him."

"Before *I* call him?"

"I'll call Mr. Richman tomorrow and see what he thinks of the idea. I'm sure he'll be willing to increase the budget for an endorsement contract with someone like—"

Cassie grabbed Erica's arm. "Back the bus up, will you? What do you mean, before *I* call him?"

Erica blinked. "You always arrange for the models."

"Models, yes. Endorsement contracts, no."

"Hmm. I see your point. All right, you get him here, and I'll get his signature on the contract."

"I don't even know where he lives!"

"You said he was from Colorado."

"There could be a thousand Tucker Reeves in Colorado."

Erica sighed. "Cassie, quit being difficult. Surely the rodeo in Florida has some record of him. There might even be some national organization he's a member of."

"Cowboys Anonymous?"

Erica patted her shoulder. "That's the spirit. I'll call you tomorrow with the figures. Surely you'll have tracked him down by then. Any questions?"

"Yes." Cassie closed her eyes and groaned. "Why me?"

Tucker stomped up the three steps to the wide porch running across the back of his two-story log home. As he kicked his boots against a porch post to knock off snow, the blazing sunset caught his eye. The blending of fiery reds and oranges reminded him of sunlight glinting off an angel's hai—

"Hell."

Tucker rubbed the back of his neck in disgust.

The woman he'd met was not an angel. The reaction of his libido had driven home the fact that she was flesh and bone.

Still…

His mind couldn't seem to separate the two. Every time Cassie's name popped into his head—which it did with alarming regularity—"Angel" followed it as naturally as night follows day.

Why the hell couldn't he forget her? He hadn't even spent an hour with the woman, so why did her green eyes haunt his dreams—waking and sleeping?

This last concussion must've done more damage than he thought.

With a sigh of defeat, Tucker entered the house where the smell of beef stew welcomed him.

"That you, Tuck?" a familiar voice called.

"It's me, Eileen." He set his hat on a shelf in the mudroom, then hung his sheepskin-lined coat on a hook below. Sitting down on a ladder-back chair, he pried off his boots.

Eileen appeared in the doorway separating the mudroom and the kitchen. "You're in early."

Tucker glanced up. Except for her hairstyle and clothes, Eileen looked like Granny on the *Beverly Hillbillies*. He'd known her since he was sixteen when she and her husband, Roy, had taken him in after he'd run away from the foster care system in Texas. "Yes, ma'am."

"Lose any today?"

He shook his head. "Not a one, though there was one heifer determined to calve in the middle of Colter Creek."

"Nobody ever claimed cows are smart. You change her mind?"

"Roy threw a rope on her and convinced her to have it on the bank, then me and Jimmy brought the young'un into the barn. Jimmy's at the bunkhouse cleaning up."

"Where's that man of mine?"

"He and Mike will be in directly. There's a couple more

heifers Roy wanted to check out. If they look like they're about to drop their calves, he and Mike'll bring 'em in.''

After a brief pause, Eileen said, "Mike seems to be coming along fine, don't he?''

Tucker nodded. Mike was the newest of the two troubled teens who were Roy's current project. The foreman of the Circle Lazy Seven had the habit of taking in strays, as he'd taken in Tucker seventeen years before.

When Tucker bought his ranch, he'd hired the couple, who'd lost their own ranch, to run the Circle Lazy Seven while he was away, which was ninety percent of the year. Eileen cooked for the hands, and Roy oversaw the cow operation.

They also took in "incorrigible" teenage boys that state institutions had given up on—with Tucker's blessing and support. The Glucks wanted to take in more, but until Tucker got enough money together to build a new bunkhouse that met state codes, they were limited to two.

Eileen's wrinkled face softened. "They should bring those heifers in, anyway. Radio says there's snow blowing in tomorrow. Four inches, maybe.''

"They probably will." Tucker stood and stretched. "That stew smells mighty good. Don't suppose I could get a mouthful before I clean up?''

Eileen laughed. "You always could get food outta me. Come on. I just pulled biscuits outta the oven. You can have one of them.''

Tucker followed Eileen's diminutive figure into the kitchen like a spoiled dog and gratefully accepted a hot biscuit.

As he bit into the flaky warmth, Eileen turned to him. "Oh, remember I told you yesterday that the Professional Rodeo Cowboys Association called, wanting to know if it was all right to give your number to someone wanting to talk to you about an endorsement contract? And you said okay? Well, she called a couple of hours ago.''

Tucker lifted a brow. "*She?* Did she leave her name and number?''

"Nope. Said she was with Burch Photography in New York City."

"New York, huh? I don't know anybody in…" Tucker's heart came to a screeching halt.

Photography. Cassie. Could it be?

Hell.

Annoyed again by his mind's lack of control, he swallowed the bite of biscuit with difficulty. The remotest link brought his mind back to her.

This photographer was in New York, so it couldn't be Cassie. There'd been an unmistakable hint of a Southern accent in her lovely, lilting, angelic voi—

"Hell."

"Beg pardon?" Eileen said.

Tucker spun on his heel. "I'm gonna go take a shower. If she calls back in the next few minutes, get her number."

"Don't get testy with me, young man. I asked her to leave the number, but she insisted on paying for the call."

He halted at the door and looked over his shoulder. "I'm sorry, Eileen. I'm not mad at you. I'm just…being stupid, is all." He gave her a wry smile. "A common occurrence."

The cook shooed him out the door. "Go wash off the mud. I'll get the phone if it rings."

Tucker had succeeded in driving Cassie from his mind by the time he'd showered, dressed and walked downstairs to his office. As he sat down in his rolling leather executive chair, a shrill ring blasted the quiet office.

He picked up the receiver. "Circle Lazy Seven."

"Is Tucker Reeves in, please?"

He knew her voice instantly. "Cassie?"

There was a slight pause, then she asked, "Mr. Reeves?"

Tucker's eyes closed and his hand clutched the receiver as if it were the handle of his bull rope. "It's you."

"How did you know?" Her voice sounded breathless.

Because he'd been hearing her voice in his dreams—both waking and sleeping. "I recognized your voice."

"I see." She paused. "You did?"

He hesitated. How much should he admit?

Hell. He couldn't get her off his mind. And she called him, didn't she? "I've been thinking about you."

He heard a tiny, smothered gasp on the other end of the line, then a muttered curse, but she didn't say anything else.

He shifted the receiver to his other ear. "I guess you've been thinking about me, too. I'm glad. I thought I'd scared you off."

"You didn't scare me off. I...had a plane to catch."

"Okay. Good. Anyway, it was clever of you to call the P.R.C.A. for my number."

"P.R.C.A.?"

"Professional Rodeo Cowboys Association."

"Oh. Yes. Well, they were cautious, but helpful."

"So..."

"Yes?"

"You want to come out here for the weekend? Or should we meet somewhere in between?"

"What? I'm afraid you have the wrong idea, Mr. Reeves. This is not a personal call."

He frowned. "It isn't? Why not?"

"I have business to discuss."

"Business? I thought you made up that story to get the P.R.C.A. to give you my number. They wouldn't do it if you weren't talking major bucks."

"I am."

Tucker's eyes narrowed. He didn't like this. Not one bit. He didn't want a business relationship with Cassie. He wanted...

What? A dazzling Christmas angel? How many times was he going to let Fate trip him as he ran for what he wanted...only to land on his face?

Who needs you?

Apparently Cassie didn't...except for some business deal.

He should refuse politely and hang up the phone. Especially considering the fact she was from New York.

He'd met big-city women before. They seemed okay at first. Hell, they were soft and luscious and as anxious to hop into bed as he was. But they were easily bored. They liked the fast pace of city life—all the people, all the traffic—all the things he hated. Big-city women were afraid of horses, turned up their nose at the smell of cows, and couldn't stand the peace of a ranch longer than two days.

He should *definitely* hang up the phone.

Right now.

He cleared his throat. "So, talk."

He heard her take a deep breath. "I called to ask if you'd be interested in coming to New York to discuss an endorsement contract."

"Endorsing what?"

"I'm not at liberty to discuss the details. I'm just the photographer. Erica Simmons, an account executive for Smith-Reese Advertising, will talk to you about it when you get here. Assuming you want to come."

The tone of her voice confused him. It almost sounded as though she didn't want him to accept. But if that were true, why did she call?

Tucker rubbed his temple. An endorsement contract. Did he want to go to New York? Hell, no. He hated any town with a population over five hundred. But he did want to see Cassie.

"We will, of course, pay all your expenses," she added grudgingly.

She was trying to talk him into it though she obviously didn't want him to come. She sounded almost…scared. Was it possible she wanted the business relationship, but was scared to death of the personal one?

He knew there wasn't an ice cube's chance in hell for any kind of lasting relationship between a country boy and a city girl, but the contradictions in Cassie's manner intrigued him.

Though every self-protective bone in his body screamed at him to say no, he asked, "When?"

"Would Saturday be too soon? I know it's just a couple of days' warning, but Erica's client will be in town for the weekend and he'd like to meet you. Of course, you might want to arrive Friday to settle in."

"But I was..." Tucker thought about the Houston rodeo he planned to attend in spite of the doctor's advice. Cassie or Houston? An easy call. Besides, maybe this was God's way of telling him to listen to the doctor. His headache had receded to a dull ache, but it was still there.

"You were what?" she asked.

"Never mind. Friday's fine."

He heard her sigh, but he couldn't tell if it was a sigh of relief or regret. Before he had time to ask, she told him about a flight out of Denver the next afternoon.

"I'll arrange for a limo to take you from the airport to the hotel," she said.

"Aren't you going to meet me?"

"Well, no. I wasn't planning on it."

Tucker frowned. How bad did she want him to come? "Plan on it. If you're not there, I'm on the next plane home."

He half expected her to say "Fine" and hang up. Instead, she released an exasperated huff and said, "All right, I'll meet you."

"Good."

"Fine. Goodbye."

"'Bye, Angel. See you soon." As the line went dead, he added, "And if you think you're going to avoid me while I'm there, you've got about ten more thinks coming."

Cassie hit the Off button on her portable phone. She stared at it as if she could see through the wires to the man in Colorado. She could still hear his deep, drawling voice calling her "Angel." He sounded so intimate, so engrossed, as if she were the center of his universe...

No!

She slammed the phone onto the coffee table and jumped to her feet. She was not going to fall into that age-old trap. The only person she'd ever meant so much to was her little brother Jason, and that was a long time ago.

She'd grown up. If she wanted such single-minded devotion, she'd get a dog. She didn't want to be important to anyone. She'd built a successful career and life during the past nine years—without a man. Without anyone but herself.

She refused to act like her mother, who needed all the attention focused on herself, who immediately looked around for another man to supply that attention when the latest one left. And they always left. Men were never around when you needed them.

Cassie had promised herself early in life that she would never depend on anyone but herself. And she'd kept that promise.

Now Tucker Reeves had popped up in her life. Twice! Like an irritating jack-in-the-box. And he obviously wanted more than an endorsement contract—demanding she meet him at the airport. Couldn't the man take a cab into the city like a normal person?

She refused to be this cowboy's nursemaid. Erica had already reserved a room for him at a hotel a few blocks away. After depositing him there, the only times Cassie planned to see him were from behind a camera. Let Erica entertain him.

But the thought of Erica "entertaining" Tucker made Cassie feel like scratching the urbane brunette's eyes out—which scared her more than anything. The feeling reeked of possessiveness. It meant she was a lot more interested than she would admit, much more than she wanted to be.

Damn!

Cassie strode to the window and stared blindly out one of the tall glass panes of her refurbished warehouse loft on the lower West Side. She'd come a long way since arriving in the Big Apple nine years ago, a skinny kid from the South with nothing going for her but a talent for taking pictures. She wasn't about to lose any part of it—or herself—over a set of broad shoulders and a thick Western drawl.

This was just her libido reacting. Pheromones colliding with testosterone. She recognized the symptoms, even if they were a lot stronger than with the football player in high school and the performance artist three years ago. The attraction she'd felt for those men died within weeks. This one would, too. She just had to resist this sweet-talking cowboy until that happened.

She had a job that consumed her time. She didn't have time for anything else. She didn't want anything else.

So what if the sound of his voice melted her bones. So, she was probably going to be spending a lot of time in his company for the next few days or even weeks.

That didn't mean she had to do anything about it. She could just be cool, stay calm, not sweat, and he'd be gone.

That's what men were good at—leaving. This one wasn't any different. She just had to remember that and she'd be fine.

Just fine.

Chapter Three

"**Y**ou want to come for a visit?" The sleeve of transparencies Cassie had been studying dropped to the light table with a soft *thwak*. Suddenly her kid brother Jason had all her attention. "Now?"

"Actually— Don't say no until you hear me out, okay?" Jason heaved a dramatic thirteen-year-old kind of sigh. "I want to live with you."

"*Live* with me? Where in the world did you get such a crazy idea?"

"I knew you'd act this way," he whined. "Nobody wants me. You don't. Mom doesn't. Maybe I should just run away from home."

"You will *not*."

Cassie brought her shock under control. *Nobody wants me* was a stage Jason went through every time their mother acquired a new husband—which she did with alarming regularity. She'd married Number Eight—Cassie had begun calling them by their number—only two months ago.

This was not the first time Jason had threatened to run away, but it was the first time he'd suggested he move in with her.

Things must be worse than Cassie had feared they might be when she'd met Number Eight at the wedding.

"You can't run away from home. Who'd keep you in computer games?"

He didn't laugh at her joke.

Cassie sighed. "You know I love you, Jason. You spend several months of the year with me. We e-mail every day I'm at home, and I talk to you several times a week."

"Then, I can come?"

"Now is not a good time, kiddo. I'm sorry. I have this extremely important job I'm working on and—"

"You always have an 'extremely important job' you're working on."

"Jason, please…"

Her brother changed tactics. "I won't be any trouble, Cassie. I promise. Please! Henry hates me. He yells at me all the time."

Cassie could hear the tears Jason was manfully trying to hide from her. She knew exactly how he felt. She'd gone through five stepfathers before she left to start a career in New York. So she didn't mouth some platitude about Jason's claim not being true. It probably was. Number Eight didn't seem as though he had the patience to deal with a thirteen-year-old boy with low self-esteem.

"I'm sorry, Jason. This isn't something I can decide right now."

"He almost…hit me today, Cassie."

She closed her eyes against his whispered pain. "What about school?"

"I can go to school with Sam. And his mom said I could stay with them when you have an out-of-town assignment— like I did last summer."

Sam was a friend Jason had made on a visit to New York a few years back. They kept up with each other through e-mail in between Jason's visits.

"Please, Cassie."

She slumped on the high stool and pressed a finger against the bridge of her nose. She didn't need this now. Tucker Reeves arrived tomorrow afternoon, and she was going to need all of her wits to deal with him.

"Give me two weeks, okay? You can fly up for a visit during spring break and we'll discuss it then."

"But, Cassie—"

"That's the best I can do right now, Jason. Take it or leave it."

"I guess I have to take it, then, don't it?" He gave another dramatic sigh, then muttered, "But that doesn't mean I have to like it."

The plane from Denver had just landed when Cassie arrived at the gate. She leaned against the floor-to-ceiling window that looked out on the runway and watched it approach.

A tall, broad-shouldered cowboy was somewhere on that plane. Was he standing up, gathering his things, or did he wait patiently for other passengers to retrieve their overhead luggage?

She'd bet on the former. Tucker Reeves did not seem like a patient man. Not when it came to getting what he wanted.

She turned when she heard the fuss at the gate behind her. Erica had reserved a first-class ticket for Tucker, so Cassie was not surprised to see a cowboy hat right behind the first passengers coming through.

He paused as he cleared the door.

Suddenly air refused to enter Cassie's lungs. She'd studied his picture during the past few days, but two-dimensional film didn't have the potency of Tucker Reeves in the flesh. Half a head and a hat above everyone else, he had a body men spend hours in gyms trying to develop.

His broad shoulders were covered by a red, white and blue Western shirt and narrowed down to a trim waist where a gold oblong belt buckle drew her eyes. His jeans weren't skintight, but they hugged slim hips and long, muscular legs that ended in well-worn brown leather boots. He held a denim-and-sheepskin jacket over one shoulder and a duffel bag in his other hand. The blue eyes that contrasted sharply with his sun-darkened skin scanned the crowd.

He oozed self-confidence and every woman around responded to it, craning their necks to watch him.

And why not? What woman didn't fantasize about having her very own cowboy? Cassie had done enough fantasizing about this one to know. Too bad she couldn't turn her fantasy into reality.

Unfortunately, he was flesh and blood, so he wouldn't disappear when the fantasy was over. There'd be all that messy relationship stuff to deal with. And a relationship was really low on her list of priorities—right under having her hair torn out by the roots.

Then his gaze locked with hers and Cassie forgot other people existed. A lazy smile showed his white teeth, adding even more contrast to his face.

He started forward. When his eyes finally released hers to glide down her body, air whooshed into her lungs, making her realize she'd forgotten to breathe. She suddenly wished she'd worn her clingy teal silk shirt instead of a bulky sweater.

He stopped three feet away. She could feel his eyes traveling over her face as surely as if his fingers touched her.

"Damn. You're prettier than I remembered." He took one more step, dropped his bag and his coat on top of it, then pulled her against him.

Before she could protest, his mouth descended on hers.

For a brief moment Cassie responded. His clean, male scent mixed faintly with coffee. His hard muscles flexed beneath her fingers. His warm body pressed against hers. He overpowered her senses, just as he had in the hospital last week. With a word and a touch, he changed her habitual coolness into mind-numbing heat.

The realization frightened her enough to drag her lips from his.

"What are you doing?" she asked in low, tight tones.

When he still didn't get the message, she pushed until he let go.

Dazed puzzlement shadowed his eyes. "Angel, if you don't know what I'm doing, you've got a lot to learn."

"I've got a lot to learn?" She poked a finger at him, stopping an inch short of his hard chest. "You're the one who needs a lesson—in manners. This is neither the time nor the place for that kind of thing."

He looked around deliberately. "I see people kissing all over."

"Not like that they're not."

One long arm curled around her waist, and he gave her a look intended to melt her bones. "Then show me how it should be done. I'm willing to learn manners if you're the teacher."

He nearly succeeded. She leaned into him an instant before she realized what he was doing.

"No!" She pushed him an arm's length away. "Let's get a few things straight, cowboy. I didn't invite you here as...well, for personal reasons. This is strictly business. I have no interest in you as a man."

Tucker pushed his hat back and planted his hands on his hips. "Liar. I watched you watch me walk over. Your eyes were eating me up like I was a big stick of candy."

Cassie gasped. *Had she been so obvious?* "I did not."

"And your lips told a different story just a minute ago. You liked kissing me...until your brain got in the way."

She closed her eyes against the truth. Damn him for being so perceptive. "All right, I liked it." Her eyes flew open as he touched her. She slapped his hand away. "But that doesn't mean I want to do it again."

"Liar," he said softly.

"Your first lesson in manners is to stop calling people liars."

"I speak the truth as I see it. If that's bad manners, then I'm rude."

"I just want to make it clear on the front end that this trip is strictly business. No kissing, no touching, no suggestive comments. All right?"

Tucker stared at her so long and so hard Cassie's palms began to sweat. "Do you agree, Mr. Reeves?"

"Hell, no."

Cassie blinked. "But you—"

He grabbed her hand and his things, then dragged her down the corridor.

Cassie struggled to regain possession of her hand until she realized how many stares were directed at them.

"Where are you going?" she hissed.

He didn't say anything until they reached an empty gate with a corner partially hidden by the check-in counter. He pulled her to the seats along the window and commanded, "Sit."

"What are you—"

"Sit."

"If you'd just tell me what—"

"Sit."

They glared at each other until he rolled his eyes. "Please."

"Oh, all right." Cassie sat, then looked up at him expectantly.

Tucker couldn't think with those suspicious green eyes boring into his, so he walked the length of the row and stared at the activity on the runway.

Old Man Fate had pulled a good one this time. Tucker had been hoping to walk off the plane into Cassie's arms. But Cassie was about as warm as a January wind.

Who needs you?

The words drifted back over the years, stinging anew.

He rubbed the back of his neck.

Cassie sure didn't seem to.

But he hadn't flown two thousand miles just to turn around

and walk onto another plane. Not without doing everything within his power to convince her to make him want to stay.

He turned to find her watching him, as wary as a wild mare haltered for the first time. Her obvious fear made him frown, and he folded his long body into the seat facing hers. He wanted to pull her onto his lap and assure her he wouldn't hurt her, but he instinctively knew that at this point, any touch would send her packing.

He took a deep breath. "First of all, my name is Tucker. The only people who call me Mr. Reeves are my newest ranch hands. Got that?"

She leaned back in her seat with a huff. "All right. I'll call you Tucker."

He nodded. "Second. I don't give a hoot in hell what your business is. It's not what I came for. I came so you and I could get to know each other. I'm perfectly willing to listen to your business proposition as long as I get what I want." He held up a hand as she gasped. "Now don't go getting riled. I didn't say I want to cart you off to bed and keep you there."

She lifted one red brow. "Now it's my turn to call you a liar."

His face twisted wryly. "Okay, that's a bald-faced lie. I want to drag you off to the nearest bed and keep you there for the next two weeks."

Crimson splashed across her cheeks, and her lips parted with the slightest of gasps.

So he added, "But I have sense enough to know that's not going to happen."

"So you do have *some* sense. I was beginning to wonder."

"There's no call getting catty on me."

"Mr. Reeves, you have not yet heard the beginning of catty."

"Tucker."

She rolled her eyes. "Tucker."

"So…you agree?"

"To what? I haven't agreed to anything."

"To us getting to know each other."

She regarded him suspiciously. "And just what will that entail?"

He spread his hands. "Why don't we start with me buying you supper?"

"Mr. Ree—" She stopped abruptly when he glowered at her.

"*Tucker.* I'm on an expense account. I'll be paying for all your meals. If you have a problem with that, then..." She spread her own hands in a mock imitation of him.

Tucker frowned. Normally he'd never let a woman pay for anything, but since the money wasn't coming out of her pocket.... "No problem. As long as we're spending time together, I don't care where we go or who pays for what."

She seemed irritated. Evidently she'd counted on his macho pride to excuse herself from the entire situation. Well, she had a lot to learn about cowboys...and about him. Cowboys were notorious for their pride, but they were nothing if not practical. And although Tucker had his share of cowboy pride, he'd never been one who cut off his nose to spite his face.

"So...you agree?" he asked.

She lowered her head and pressed a finger to the bridge of her nose.

"Well?" he asked after a moment.

"I'm thinking."

"Looks like it hurts."

He grinned at the glare she sent him until she had to fight a smile.

She heaved a melodramatic sigh to cover her struggle. "I don't have a choice, do I?"

"You always have a choice."

She shook her head. "Not if I want to avoid being screamed at by Erica."

"Erica?"

"She's the account rep for Smith-Reese Advertising—the agency you'll be working for."

"Ah. Your client."

"Yes."

"A valuable one?"

"Yes. Very."

"I see." He pushed his hat back on his head and leaned forward. "I just remembered. I have one condition."

"Another one?"

He ignored her sarcasm. "You have to do this willingly. I want to know you're going to give this a genuine shot. If I'm going to be riled up every time I'm with you, there isn't much point."

"Or?"

"Or I get on a plane back to Colorado. Right now."

"In other words, you're forcing yourself down my throat...and I have to like it."

He hated the way she put it. "I'm not forcing anything on you."

"Yes, you are."

After considering her reply for a moment, he nodded, then rose slowly and picked up his bag.

"What are you doing?" she asked sharply.

He tipped his hat. "So long, ma'am. Thanks for the ride."

"You can't go home." She sprang to her feet and grabbed his arm.

Sparks seemed to fly from where she touched him. Tucker turned back to see if she'd been affected, as well. The way her eyes widened and the way she instantly let go told him she felt the shock as much as he did.

"Why?" he demanded.

She stared at his arm as if it were a snake about to strike. Then she lifted her wide green eyes to his. "Why what?"

He smiled faintly. "Why can't I go home?"

"Oh." She swallowed hard. "Why can't you go home."

"Are you going to deny you felt it, too?"

"Felt what?"

"For crying out—" He dropped his bag and grabbed her shoulders. "This."

He pressed his lips to hers in a kiss that fell just short of bruising. He wanted her. Badly. Most of all, he wanted to make her admit how much she wanted him.

It didn't take long. Within seconds she wrapped her arms around his neck and pressed her body into his.

Tucker rewarded her immediately by softening the kiss, drawing it out, turning hot and punishing into slow and sensual. He didn't stop until she moaned.

He leaned his forehead against hers. "Will you admit it now?"

"Admit what?"

He loved the way she became mindless when he touched her. He couldn't remember a woman ever doing that. "At the very least, admit you could spend time with me and not hate it."

Her eyes cleared immediately. She winced and lowered her head. "Do I have to?"

He lifted her chin with one finger. "Yes."

"You'll stay if I do?"

"You'd better believe it, Angel."

"I want to make a personal protest here."

"Go right ahead."

"You use guerrilla tactics, and I think you're mean."

He smiled. "Complaint noted."

"Keep that in mind."

"I will. And, Cassie?"

"Yes?"

"I want to kiss you again."

She shivered. "Tucker?"

"Yes?"

"The limo's waiting."

"Cassie?"

"Yes?"

"I don't care."

Then he showed her how much he did.

Chapter Four

"Perfume? You want me to sell perfume?"

Cassie glanced at Mr. Richman and Erica, who were clearly taken aback by Tucker's horrified tone. They sat in the corner of Diane's—a ritzy restaurant fifty-seven floors above Times Square. Through the floor-to-ceiling windows they had a spectacular view of the city.

"Technically, it's cologne, Tucker," Mr. Richman said patiently. "We don't sell perfume for men."

"What's the difference? It's all smelly stuff, isn't it?"

"Well, yes, but—"

"What did you think we had in mind, Tucker?" Erica asked smoothly.

Tucker threw his hands wide. "Hell, I didn't have any idea. Hats, boots, jeans. Something that makes sense for a cowboy to slap his name on."

"But you're a perfect representative for this particular product," the ad exec argued. "It's called *Lasso*. The target market is all those urban cowboys out there who spend their weekends line dancing. We've run the demographics and our research shows—"

"Line dancing? You telling me I've got to dance in a stupid line?"

Cassie smothered a smile at the shock on Tucker's face. People not part of the conversation might think Erica had asked him to stand still and take the charge of a crazed bull.

"Well, actually, I hadn't thought of that, but why not? Cassie, what do you think, visually?"

"Well…"

"Nope. No way. If you did so much research, you'd have found out that real cowboys don't line dance." Tucker leaned back in his chair. "And they do not wear perfume. Or cologne or whatever the hell you call it."

For a long moment the three of them stared at the rugged face for once not shadowed by a cowboy hat. Even without it, nobody could mistake Tucker for anything but a cowboy. The contrast between him and Daniel Richman was as stark as the contrast between Tucker and the cityscape stretching out behind him.

Cassie had seen this implacable look on Tucker's face several times already—at the airport and when he insisted on seeing her to her apartment last night. She'd expected another assault on her senses, but he just kissed her cheek, made her lock her door, and left.

She wasn't disappointed. No way. But she'd felt…cheated.

"Line dancing isn't a very good visual, anyway, not for still photography," Cassie said. "Television would be a different story."

Erica shook her head. "TV's not in the mix right now. We think we can have a greater impact with print ads."

She looked at her client for corroboration. Mr. Richman nodded.

"The look we're going for here, in my opinion, is something totally different from line dancing," Cassie continued. "Even though the target market does line dance, in their dreams they'd rather be riding a bull or roping a calf. Isn't that why they have those mechanical bulls in those country dancing places? These guys want the image of the cowboy, not necessarily the life. That's what we're selling, isn't it? The image?"

Mr. Richman nodded. "Exactly."

Erica gave in graciously. "All right, line dancing is out. What kind of shots did you have in mind?"

"I think we should let him be Tucker Reeves, Rodeo Star. Only him in the picture, no other distractions. Just a lasso and a cowboy and all his animal magnetism."

Erica pursed her lips, then nodded. "I can see that."

"Aren't you forgetting one thing here?" Tucker interrupted. "I don't wear perfume, and I'm not about to start."

Erica waved an elegant hand at him. "No one said you have to actually wear the cologne. After all, smell doesn't come through on film, now does it?"

"But the advertisements would make folks think I wear it, wouldn't they?" he demanded.

"Well, yes, I suppose they would."

He crossed his arms over his chest. "Can't do it. I'm the current World Champion Bull Rider. I have an obligation to uphold a certain reputation. A cowboy reputation. And cowboys don't wear cologne."

"Why not?" Erica asked. "Does it attract flies? Does it scare the cows?"

Tucker shrugged. "Hell if I know. Probably because most cowboys can't afford it. Some of that stuff costs as much as a new saddle."

Erica's eyes sparkled and Cassie knew she was going in for the kill. She would feel sorry for Tucker if she wasn't certain he could hold his own.

"If you take this job, Tucker, you'll be able to afford any cologne you want." The ad exec then named a sum that made the cowboy whistle.

Tucker's wide eyes looked at Erica, then at Mr. Richman who sat quietly with his fingertips steepled, then back to the ad exec.

"You're yanking my rope, right?" Tucker asked.

Erica smiled and shook her head.

"Hell, to make that much money I'd have to place in every P.R.C.A.-sponsored rodeo in the U.S. of A."

Erica just kept smiling. She'd done her homework well. Cassie was only a little surprised at how much they were offering. Top professional models drew that much and more. But even though Tucker hadn't modeled a day in his life, he had something much better—a name and a reputation that could sell the product.

"Does the amount make the decision a little easier?" Erica asked.

"Hell, no. Makes it twice as hard."

The ad exec laughed and Mr. Richman joined her.

"Take time to think it over, Tucker," Erica suggested. "See the sights. The limo's at your disposal. If you need a guide, I'm sure I can arrange—"

"Cassie's going to take me sight-seeing," Tucker announced, placing his hand over the one she'd rested on the arm of her chair.

Cassie felt heat rise from her neck to her hairline. Tucker's hand on hers made her feel exposed, and she desperately wanted to pull away, but didn't.

Erica's eyebrows shot up. She looked so surprised and pleased, Cassie barely refrained from rolling her eyes. She knew she'd have to explain to Erica sooner or later.

"Excellent," Erica said with enthusiasm. "Cassie knows the city almost as well as a native. I'm sure you'll have a great time." She glanced around the table. "If we're ready, I'm sure you two want to get started sight-seeing."

Tucker rose and pulled out Cassie's chair. "Thanks for the grub."

"It's our pleasure," Erica crooned.

They parted at the entrance to the restaurant, but not before Erica managed to whisper in Cassie's ear, "I've lassoed him, now you pull him in. I've got a press conference scheduled for Sunday afternoon.''

Tucker looked down from a viewing deck of the Empire State Building. From this vantage point, the Big Apple resembled nothing more than a giant ant colony with millions of the little critters swarming up and down every thoroughfare.

Far from feeling a thrill at being part of the action, Tucker felt worlds apart. With so many people crowded onto a tiny island, how could just one matter?

Who needs you?

He drew up the collar of his coat and pulled his eyes away from the view...to a better one.

Cassie stood beside him, her attention focused on the panorama. A cold breeze lifted strands of hair escaping from her braid. The setting sun set her hair on fire and added a pink tinge to her smooth ivory skin.

He sure as hell didn't want to spend another minute in a city that made him feel insignificant, but this woman made it worth putting up with. Though he knew it was unintentional on her part, she made him feel needed.

Yes, Cassie needed him. And for more than just a photography job. Her need for him certainly wasn't obvious. She made damn sure of that. It was something he felt instinctively, but couldn't quite pin down—which only served to irritate him.

If he knew the exact nature of her need, he might be able to fill it so thoroughly, she'd look at him with something besides panic in her eyes.

He pondered that possibility, finally deciding there was only one way to find out. He had to get to know her better—and let her know him.

"So, you're not from New York originally?"

She turned to him in faint surprise. He'd purposefully kept the conversation focused on the sights of New York, not avoiding personal questions but not asking them, either. She'd done her part as tour guide, not once mentioning *Lasso* or the reasons why he should consider their deal.

He respected her for that. It made him like her even more.

"No," she answered. When he regarded her expectantly, she continued grudgingly, "I'm not from anywhere, really. I was born in a little town in Georgia, but I've lived all over the southeast—Alabama, Tennessee, Florida."

"A military brat?" he asked.

"My mother moved us from town to town." Cassie reached for the camera hanging perpetually around her neck and aimed it at him.

Tucker placed his hand over the lens. "Don't hide behind that thing."

Cassie lowered the camera with a surprised look. Then she frowned and turned to move further down the railing. She didn't say anything else.

As Tucker followed, he was certain she wasn't telling him the whole story. "How did you end up in New York?"

She glanced at him, then away. "It was a conscious decision. There's a song that says if you can make it here, you can make it anywhere. I wanted to make it here as a photographer."

"And you did."

She smiled. "Yes, I did. I also wanted to get out of the South, especially small towns. I wanted to go where women are taken seriously. Where you aren't an object of pity if you don't have a husband."

"You have something against husbands?"

She gave him an enigmatic look, then strolled over to the north side of the viewing area.

Because of the cold breeze, they were almost alone on the outside deck. The few people there stared at Tucker, and he could hear the word "cowboy" in the buzz of their conversations. One Oriental man even snapped a picture of Tucker instead of the view.

Feeling like a freak show act, he pulled down the brim of his hat and followed Cassie around the deck.

Cassie felt Tucker come up beside her. If he was going to get personal, then she felt free to do the same. "Have you thought about Erica's proposal?"

His blue eyes delved deep into hers, then he looked away. "Yes, ma'am."

"And?"

"It's a helluva lot of money."

"Yes, it is."

"I've been needing to build a new bunkhouse on my ranch."

"This would surely be enough for that."

He leaned a hip against the wall and placed a boot on the step of a telescope. "Trying to talk me into it?"

Cassie shrugged. "I suppose so."

"What do you get out of it?"

She looked away from his intent gaze. "Just my usual fee. But I'll get that no matter who poses for the ads."

"Then why? You certainly can't say you want to keep me around for my own sake. I make you too uncomfortable."

Cassie stared blindly at the strip of green in the distance that was Central Park. Tucker was wrong. He made her entirely too comfortable. She'd enjoyed their afternoon more than she'd enjoyed anything in a long time. Being with Tucker was fun. And seemed right...somehow.

In the process of digging for the numerous faults she was certain he was hiding, she'd discovered she actually liked him. She liked his sense of humor and his smile, his deep, drawling voice and his quiet solicitousness. Tucker seemed like a man she could depend on—but she knew it was an illusion. "Dependable man" was an oxymoron.

No, he didn't make her uncomfortable. He confused her—more than anything in her life.

So why was she trying to talk him into taking the job? If

he took it, he'd be staying several weeks. If he didn't take it, he'd leave. She'd probably never see him again.

The rising panic that realization caused told her exactly why she was trying to talk him into accepting. There was something here she wanted to hold on to—for just a little longer. She knew if he left now, she'd regret it for a long, long time.

She couldn't tell him that, however, so she settled for a half-truth. "This deal means a lot to Erica. And Erica means a lot to me. She helped me when I first came to New York. Gave me my first real job. Taught me about the advertising business."

"Is she the only reason?"

"Well, I think you'd be sensational in the ads. You have a kind of..."

"Animal magnetism?" he supplied with a grin.

She smiled back. He had a memory like an elephant. "Exactly. Erica noticed it the instant she saw your pictures."

"Pictures? The ones where I was hightailing it away from ol' Crazy Eight?"

"Yes, but I also took several earlier. I used a telephoto lens, so I'm sure you didn't see me. You were standing with a group of cowboys. There was one shot especially. Somebody must've called to you because you glanced up and smiled, almost as if you were looking directly into the camera. It was quite...well, let's just say you took Erica's breath away—and that's not easy to do."

He gave her that same smile. "Sexy, huh?"

"With a capital S-E-X."

He leaned closer and lowered his voice. "Did you think so?"

Cassie's nails bit into her palm. She'd had too many years of avoiding personal conversations to give him a simple yes. So she fell back behind defensive walls by avoiding the question. "The ads will appear in magazines like *GQ* and *Esquire*. Probably in a few women's magazines, too. Cowboys don't read those kinds of publications, do they?"

The look on his face told her she'd disappointed him. Feeling like an utter failure and hating it, she took a breath to answer his earlier question, but his own answer saved her.

"Cowboys don't, but their wives read magazines. Ranching gets mighty lonesome in some parts, especially for the women. Reading is a major source of entertainment for a lot of them, magazines included." He shook his head. "I can't make this decision on the off chance the rodeo world won't find out about it. If it's going to be a national campaign like you said, somebody will see it and tell someone else who'll tell someone else until they all know."

"What will you base your decision on?"

He shrugged. "The money, I guess, and..."

Her eyes narrowed. "And what?"

He smiled faintly. "And you."

Cassie wished she hadn't pushed him. Basing his decision on her made it sound as if she were important to him. The possibility made her feel warm from the inside out, but that would mean she gave a damn one way or the other. Which she didn't. Being independent meant you had no ties of any kind—even ties of the heart. *Especially* not ties of the heart.

He frowned when she didn't answer, then shifted his gaze to the city. "I've seen enough of the view, if you're ready to go."

An elevator was unloading, so they walked right on. Tucker pulled Cassie around to stand in front of him and kept his hands at her waist.

From that instant on, she was only vaguely aware of the other people on the elevator. She could feel Tucker's breath tickling the back of her head and the warmth of his hands through several layers of clothes.

She'd forgotten how intimate such simple touches could be.

They stepped onto the street, where the limo waited for them at the curb. After making their way inside, they sat quietly and let the driver fight the traffic.

By the time they crossed Broadway, Cassie missed Tucker's deep, rumbling voice. "What are you thinking about?"

"The Circle Lazy Seven."

"Your ranch?"

He nodded. "Roy and Eileen sure would be tickled if I came home with enough money to build the bunkhouse they've been hankering after."

"So..."

He hesitated a moment, then said, "Okay, I'll do it. It's good money for honest work. No one can complain about that."

"You will? Good. I'll call Erica from the restaurant. She'll hit the moon."

He nodded.

"You'll sign the contract at a press conference on Sunday, and we'll start shooting Monday, if that's okay."

He shrugged. "Why not?"

"Will it interfere with your rodeo schedule?"

He smiled wryly. "No."

"Well, then...good. Everybody gets what they want."

"Not quite."

"Oh?" Then his meaning hit her. "Oh."

His gaze bored into hers. "I haven't kissed you all day."

She sucked in a quick breath, which she knew he heard. Damn him. He always caught her off guard with his plain talking. "So?"

"So I'm dying to. Do you think we'd shock the driver?"

An opaque glass separating them from the driver began to rise.

Tucker started. "What the—? Is he doing that?"

Feeling pressure on her finger, Cassie glanced down. She was the one raising the partition.

She yanked her finger from the button.

Could fingers have Freudian slips?

"What's wrong?" Tucker glanced over and saw the buttons. He grinned. "Don't stop there."

"But I didn't know I…" She trailed off as he leaned across her and finished the job. "Tucker, no. We can't."

"The hell we can't." He hauled her onto his lap.

The sensation of being lifted was alien and alarming. "Tucker! No!"

"Yes, Cassie. Oh, yes."

"But we—"

"Ssshhh." He leaned her back against his right arm and stroked a strand of hair from her cheek. "The windows are tinted. No one can see."

His head lowered, and his heat wrapped around her. Cassie could feel her resistance rapidly melting and made one last-ditch effort at stopping him. "Tucker, please…"

He stopped when his lips were just a whisper away. "Please what?"

She could feel every single point where their bodies touched. Her softness molded to his hardness—especially the growing bulge against her hip. His warm breath mingled with hers, driving away the ability to think. He felt so solid, so permanent, so male.

Though she knew she shouldn't, she wanted to taste him again.

With a soft sigh of surrender, Cassie slipped her arms around his neck. "Please kiss me."

With a growl deep in his throat, Tucker pressed his mouth to hers. She opened immediately to his questing tongue.

The rush was like a teetotaler after her first shot of whiskey—heady, strong and totally overwhelming. She felt as if she were drowning in a sea of sensations so foreign she couldn't have named them even if her brain had been working.

When he worked his hand under her sweater and cupped her breast, she gasped with pleasure. Then she ripped open the snaps of his shirt to get at his chest. Delighted to find a light mat of hair covering it, she ran her fingers through the dark strands until he moaned into her mouth.

She existed in a primal state—aware of every pulse of her

blood, every breath taken in, every muscle that moved. She was aware of every beat of Tucker's heart, every caress, every moan. Yet she was oblivious to the world around them. Oblivious that there even was a world around them.

And she loved it. Every mind-numbing, thought-sucking, will-demolishing second of it.

When he pulled back for air, she followed his mouth the way a baby follows his mother's breast.

He rewarded her with another kiss, then murmured, "Cassie?"

She didn't want to rise to the surface of the primordial soup she swam in, didn't want to have to think. So she pulled his mouth back to hers.

He complied the first time, and the second. But the third time he resisted. "Cassie."

"Hmm?"

"Look at me."

"I don't want to."

She felt him smile. "Cassie?"

"Hmm?"

"We have to talk."

The intrusion was irritating—like a blaring alarm early in the morning when all you wanted to do was sleep. "But that would require thinking."

He chuckled. "Sorry about that."

She frowned. "If you want to continue this, it would be better if you didn't make me think."

Tucker tightened his arms around the warm, willing, earthy angel that had fallen from heaven into his arms. If he wanted to continue? What kind of stupid statement was that? He wanted Cassie more than he'd ever wanted any woman. The need to make her his was so acute, it was painful.

And she was right. If he gave her enough time for her brain to kick in, she would stop him. He should just go ahead and take her and get it over with. They were half undressed already, and it's what they both wanted.

He had just enough control left to know he couldn't. Not here. They were in a limo in the middle of a crowded street, for God's sake.

Damn. Why did she have to be so willing now? Why not later, when he had her alone in his room or her apartment?

She tried to pull his head down again. Her lips were moist and red and slightly swollen from his kisses.

He almost gave in.

With a regretful groan, he held back. "No, Cassie. We can't make love here."

Her eyes finally opened—wide. "Make love?"

He brushed a strand of fire from her flushed cheek. "That's where we were headed."

"But...all we did was kiss." She glanced down at his bare chest. "Okay. Maybe it was a tad more than that."

"Angel, a minute ago, you wouldn't have denied me anything."

"But I... You..." Her head fell back with a moan.

"And while I can't deny I want to make love to you, I think we need to talk first."

She winced, then straightened in his lap, pulling her bra and sweater back into place.

He allowed her to climb off his lap but didn't budge from the middle of the seat where he'd moved when he raised the partition. By the time he'd resnapped his shirt and shifted to ease the strain on his jeans, he was even closer.

She slid as far away as possible, which wasn't far. "So...talk."

He studied her lovely face, closed now where before it had been open. Her luminous green eyes regarded him warily.

"There's something here—an attraction—that neither of us can explain. Why are you fighting it?"

She sniffed. "It's just physical."

"Well, of course it's just physical. Any other kind of relationship between us doesn't stand the chance of a snowflake in hell."

She blinked, obviously startled that he'd agreed so readily. "If that's the case, you're the one fighting it. I wanted to keep going, if you'll remember."

"I stopped because we need to get this straight. There's no sense working at cross-purposes when our purpose is the same. I want you, and you want me. The question is, what are going to do about it?"

She shrugged. "Nothing."

"Hell, nothing doesn't work. We've been doing nothing about it for the past two days, and we're still fired up. Doing nothing just makes it worse."

"So what do you suggest? Have sex like rabbits while you're here?"

His face tightened as he controlled his response to the image. He cleared his throat. "Well, that's one option."

"If you think I'm going to—"

"But not the only one. If we spend time together, get to know each other, maybe we could cure ourselves of this…this…"

"Malady?" she suggested when he hesitated.

"I don't think we're sick, really. Just barking up the wrong trees. I'm a cowboy and you're a New York photographer. That ain't gonna work."

"I agree with you there, but how would getting better acquainted help?"

He leaned back. "I haven't met a woman yet who hasn't cured me of any attraction I felt toward her when I got to know her. Especially big-city women. I'm sure you won't be any different."

Cassie lifted a brow at the veiled insult, but caught the gist of his reasoning. "And I'm sure you have enough obnoxious habits to cure me of my attraction to you. Like you said, we don't know each other at all."

"Right."

"I probably won't be able to stand you after two more days in your company."

His eyes narrowed. "And I'll probably be ready to hog-tie and gag you after a week."

Cassie frowned at his words, then leaned back and considered them. He must've read her mind when he got off the plane yesterday. What he was suggesting would let her have her cake and eat it, too. Or rather, let her have her cowboy and... She squirmed against the leather seat.

Get your libido under control, Cassie.

She could have this cowboy with no messy relationship garbage to deal with. Right? Perhaps she'd better clarify that. "And since we know we're doomed from the beginning, we won't have any expectations."

He nodded. "No talk about the future, 'cause there isn't any."

"You won't begin to tell me how to run my life—"

"And you won't tell me how to run mine."

Cassie felt her muscles begin to relax. "It sounds so...so liberating."

"It does, doesn't it?"

"No games between us."

"Just the honest truth."

She lifted a brow. Honesty? That would be novel in a man. She decided to test it. "What if our libidos get in the way?"

He shrugged. "Then we'll satisfy them, assuming we both feel the same, of course. Fires that start quick are usually over quick, but they burn real hot."

Cassie took a deep breath, trying to douse the image he brought to mind. "We'll take each moment as it comes, though."

"Fair enough."

She nodded and flexed her hands. Did she dare risk it? The idea was as seductive as his smile. To be the focus of this cowboy's attention, to be the center of his universe for just a few weeks—or until she no longer wanted to be, whichever came first.

Why not? It not only sounded liberating, it sounded like fun.

Before she could change her mind, she offered him her hand. "It's just crazy enough to work. Shall we shake on it?"

"Hell, no." His hand swallowed hers, and he pulled her back onto his lap. "Bargains like this should be sealed with a kiss."

"Again?" Cassie took in a quick, hard breath as his warmth surrounded her. "I don't think—"

"Don't think," he urged softly, his lips hovering just out of reach. "That's what this is all about. We don't have to think about anything, we just do what feels right."

"Until we no longer feel anything," she whispered.

"Right."

Then his mouth touched hers, and she was no longer capable of thought. Heat flowed from his lips directly into her bloodstream, burning through her body like quick-fire.

"Open your lips for me, Angel."

"I—"

As soon as her lips parted, his tongue slid inside.

He groaned, and Cassie felt the deep rumblings against her side. Kissing Tucker felt so right, so inevitable. She dragged her teeth across his lower lip.

He wrenched his head away. "Damn!"

She opened her eyes, feeling dazed. "Did I hurt you?"

"Yes. No. Damn." He glanced out the window, then ran his eyes over her face. "I really hate to tell you this, but we're at the restaurant."

Cassie looked over her shoulder, then groaned.

"I reckon we should go in," Tucker said.

"I guess we should."

"I don't reckon you'd be willing to pick up where we left off…later."

Cassie clenched her hand to keep her fingernails from raking along the stubble on his chin. "Like we said earlier—one minute at a time."

* * *

Tucker was a perfect gentleman during dinner and the ride home. He was a charming companion, Cassie discovered, as he told her stories about the rodeo life that made her laugh and gasp and call him crazy.

As he had the night before, he insisted on walking her to her door.

She opened it, walked in and turned to face him. "It's still early. Would you like to come in for some coffee?"

She hadn't meant the question to sound like a provocative invitation, but as soon as the words were out, she remembered what he'd said about picking up where they'd left off. She was more than willing. In fact, she was ready to drag him into the apartment if he didn't come in quickly.

Tucker's blazing blue eyes searched hers. "Are you sure?"

She cleared her throat. "Am I sure of what? If I have coffee? I'm fairly certain I do, but if you're not going to stay if I don't, then—"

He cut her off with a kiss.

With a sigh, Cassie leaned into him. Finally she could scratch the itch that had bothered her for a week—ever since meeting this tall, handsome cowboy. Once the itch was gone, she'd be over him and could go on with her work, as happy and content as she was before.

Tucker slammed the door closed with one boot, his mouth never losing contact with hers. He had been bending to kiss her, but now straightened, lifting her off the floor.

"Which way?" he murmured.

"At the end of the—"

"Cassie? That's you, isn't it?"

Tucker spun as the call echoed down the hardwood floors.

Cassie gasped as a form stepped into the hall, silhouetted by the light from the guest bedroom. In shock, she slid down Tucker's body until her feet struck the floor. "Jason?"

Chapter Five

Cassie gaped at her brother's dark form. "What are you do-ing here?"

Tucker flicked on the lights.

Jason stood in the middle of the hall, dressed in baggy jeans and a Grateful Dead T-shirt. His dark brown hair had been buzz-cut halfway up his skull and left several inches long on top with a blunt cut all the way around.

"Nice to see you, too." His gaze shifted from her to Tucker and narrowed to the point of belligerence.

How much had he seen? She took a step forward to draw his attention. "Jason, answer me. What are you doing in New York?"

"I told you I had to come," he said.

"But—" She was having trouble comprehending that her thirteen-year-old brother who belonged in Macon, Georgia, was standing in her New York apartment. "How did you get here? Does Mother know where you are?"

Instead of answering, Jason looked at Tucker. "Who's this guy?"

Cassie glanced back at Tucker, who watched them with a

guarded expression. Jason had never seen Cassie with any man before, much less one who looked as out of place as a guppy in a goldfish bowl. "Jason, this is Tucker Reeves. He'll be modeling for the extremely important job I told you about. Tucker, this is my brother, Jason Warner. He has a different last name because…well, it's a long story."

Tucker stepped around her and offered his hand to Jason.

Jason made no move to take it.

"Jason, don't be rude," Cassie said.

The boy deliberately crammed his hands into his pants' pockets.

Cassie's jaw dropped. She'd never seen Jason so rude to anyone. "Jason, you will apologize to Mr. Reeves this instant."

Jason stuck out his chin.

Tucker faced Cassie. "I'll get out of your way." He gave Jason a stiff nod over his shoulder. "Nice to meet you."

"Right…cowboy."

As Tucker moved toward the door, Cassie punched her brother's shoulder. "What is wrong with you? I've never seen you like this. You will apologize or I'll—"

"You'll what?"

Cassie's hand itched to slap the challenge from his face. When had her brother turned into a…a teenager? "I'll put you on the next plane back to Macon."

Concern wiped most of the combativeness from Jason's face. Still, his tone was less than gracious when he said, "Sorry, man."

Tucker turned with his hand on the doorknob and gave Jason a brief nod. "Sure." He gave Cassie a sympathetic look. "Good night, Angel."

"Just a minute." She turned to her brother. "Go back to your room, please. I'll be in to straighten this out in a minute."

"But you—"

"Go." She pointed toward the guest room door. "Arguing is not in your best interest right now, brother dear."

Jason gave Tucker one last hateful look, then spun on his heel. He stomped back to the bedroom he used while staying in New York and slammed the door.

Shaking her head in disbelief, Cassie turned to find Tucker's gaze on her, warm, sympathetic.

"He's every bit as ornery as the boys Roy takes in," he said softly.

She sighed. "I don't know what his problem is. I still can't believe he's here. But I need to find out why, so I guess you'd better go."

He nodded. "I understand. Believe me, I've been there for the fireworks. Tough love is hard. You don't want any witnesses, and he doesn't, either."

"What do you mean, 'tough love'? I don't believe in violence."

"Tough love doesn't necessarily mean taking off your belt, Cassie. The best thing anyone could do for that boy is throw him on the back of a bronc and let them pound the meanness out of each other."

"Oh, shucks. They just ran out of wild broncs down at Macy's." She set her hands on her hips. There was more difference between them than city girl/country boy. Better to realize it now before she made a huge mistake. Still... somehow...the realization hurt. "I don't know what cave you crawled out of, cowboy, but *civilized* people find peaceful ways to solve problems."

His eyes narrowed. "If you mean New Yorkers, give me cowboys any day."

Her chin lifted. "I'll see you tomorrow at the press conference."

"Won't you be picking me up?"

"I'd better not. I'll probably have to bring Jason along."

He stared at her for a long minute, then left with a solid click of the latch.

Cassie threw the dead bolts on the front door, then turned. Music blared from the guest room, so loud and strident she felt it like pounding waves at the ocean.

Part of her was still shocked. That a thirteen-year-old could make his way—safely—from Macon, Georgia, to New York City was amazing. That it was the little boy she'd help raise was astounding.

Another part of her was proud of his daring and ingenuity. Still another part was furious that he would attempt something so stupid, especially after she'd told him he could come in two weeks.

The anger was what propelled her down the hall. She opened his door, marched over to the boom box he'd brought with him and flicked off the power.

Then she turned on him. "What the heck were you thinking?"

The belligerence lasted a few more seconds, then melted into sheepishness. "I dunno. I just… I couldn't stay there, Cassie. He hates me. I told you he almost hit me the other day."

"If you acted like this, I can almost understand why."

"They don't want me there. Either of them. I'm just in the way."

"Mother loves you." The words sounded weak, even to Cassie. "In her own way."

He gave a very adult snort of disbelief. "Henry doesn't."

She sighed. "No, Henry doesn't. He doesn't strike me as the kind of man who can love anyone. I wonder at his marrying Mother."

"Well, yeah, he's like fifty-six and never been married. Pigg said everyone thinks he's gay, and he married Momma to prove he isn't."

"Pigg?"

"A kid at school." Jason shrugged. "It's his last name. Swear to God."

"It still doesn't explain how you got here."

"I flew. How else?"

"From Atlanta?"

He nodded. "Caught a bus to Atlanta, then got on a direct flight. I took a cab from the airport. It was easy."

"How did you pay for the ticket?"

"Momma's credit card. She gave me one so she wouldn't have to take me shopping for clothes and junk."

"Does she know where you are?"

"I left a note on her dresser."

Cassie sat heavily on the daybed and threw her hands in the air. "What the heck am I supposed to do with you?"

"Don't make me go back, Cassie." He leaned forward, his voice plaintive. "I hate it there."

"I've got news for you, kiddo. Thirteen-year-olds hate it everywhere."

"Cassie, please! You know how it is."

Unfortunately, she did. She'd lived with five of her mother's eight husbands, including her own father who died in a hunting accident when she was three. With the exception of Jason's father—husband number four—they had gotten progressively worse. None of them seemed to want children, especially children who weren't their genetic progeny.

She rubbed the tight spot between her brows. She didn't need this right now. Her life was complicated enough with the male who had just left. The male with whom she'd just agreed to have a wild, passionate fling.

And she thought Jason had made a stupid decision.

As if they could do anything with Jason hanging around, anyway...

Cassie's head came up.

Now there's a thought. With Jason around, it would be difficult—if not impossible—for her to maintain a relationship with Tucker...which meant it would be difficult—if not impossible—for her to do something stupid. Not only would Jason require a lot of her time, but he seemed to resent Tucker—the perfect excuse for Cassie to get rid of the cowboy at the end of the day's shoot.

Heck, after a few doses of the medicine he'd just received, Tucker would be hightailing it out the door with no prodding from her.

"Cassie? Please?"

She focused on her brother's face. "We still have to get Mother's approval."

He rolled his eyes. "Like she's gonna insist on me going back."

"I'm not saying this is going to be permanent. We'll have to see how things work out. I travel a lot, you know."

"I know. Sam said I could stay with him and his mom, like I did last summer."

"Yes, well, we'll see how Mrs. Evans feels about that after a few months of it."

"It'll be okay." He rushed to the bed and hugged her. "Thank you, Cassie. You won't be sorry."

She hugged him back. It felt good—like old times. "Just remember that I can ship you home anytime. I'm not your legal guardian."

"Okay."

She ruffled his hair as he pulled away. "I guess I'd better go call Mother. If she agrees—"

"Like she's not gonna."

"If she agrees, I'll have to call Tucker and my assistants and postpone the shoot until after lunch on Monday. Hopefully, that will give us enough time to enroll you in school." She stood and headed for the door. "We'll go shopping tomorrow, before the press conference. Call Sam in the morning and find out what you need, okay?"

"I have to start school Monday?" he whined.

"Yes, you do." She turned on him, planting a hand on her hip. "You want to argue about it?"

"Yes...but I won't." Jason grinned and fell back on the bed, arms spread. "I don't care. I'm home!"

Tucker stared at the outfit Cassie's assistant held—white satin shirt and pants with fringe lining every seam. "You're yanking my stirrup, right?"

Susan shook her head. "This is what was sent over. I guess Cassie okayed it."

He shrugged and reached for the shirt. "Hell, they're paying me enough I guess I'd wear a gorilla suit."

Susan held the shirt away. "Wait. Aren't you going to shave first?"

Tucker ran a hand over his jaw. "Do I need to? I shaved two hours ago."

"Not your face, your…you know." She waved a hand in front of his chest.

Tucker's jaw dropped. "My chest? You want me to shave my chest?"

"Actually, I'm surprised they didn't send you to get it waxed days ago. Now we'll have little red bumps all ov—"

"You want me to shave my chest?" he bellowed.

She blinked. "Is there a problem? I don't know a single male model with chest hair."

"I'm not a damn model." Tucker strode to the dressing room door and shoved it open. "Cassie!"

She stood across the studio with her other assistant, Marc, stretching on her toes to adjust what looked like some sort of silver umbrella. She looked over her shoulder. "What?"

"I'm not shaving my chest!"

She murmured something to Marc, who lifted his hand to support the umbrella, and walked over to Tucker. Her eyes assessed him on the way, coldly, impersonally, as though he was a prize bull she might buy. "You're right. We'll need to have it waxed. We'll shoot around it to—"

"Hell, no, we're not having it waxed." It was bad enough that she'd abandoned him to spend yesterday alone. But he hadn't been able to argue, because she spent it getting her kid brother ready for school. The only time he'd seen her was at the zoo they'd called a press conference yesterday afternoon.

Now she acted as if she hardly knew him—and had been

ever since he walked in the door. He didn't know if it was her professional manner or if she was still mad at him for suggesting she give her kid brother a hard time.

Cassie lifted a red brow. "Calm down, Tucker. What's the big deal? All male models have their chest hair removed."

A tendon in his face quivered. "I'm not a model. And I'm not having a single hair on this chest touched. Understand?"

"How many chest hairs have you seen in pictures since...well, since Arnold Schwarzenegger made his first movie?" she replied. "And you have so much of it."

"And I intend to keep it. Every last hair. I didn't hear you complaining about it Saturday in the limo when you—"

Color shot into Cassie's cheeks. She shoved a hand over his mouth and whispered, "Hush. Everyone doesn't have to know our business."

He ran the tip of his tongue over the palm of her hand, which made her yank it away. He lifted an eyebrow. "Are you ashamed of wanting me?"

She glanced at her assistants. Marc was busy adjusting lights but Susan watched with interest. At Cassie's pointed look, Susan returned to the dressing room. When Cassie's eyes turned back to him, they held death threats. "Yes."

"So, you're still mad at me over Jason."

She threw her hands in the air. "Maybe I just don't like you."

Tucker latched onto her waist and tugged her against him. "Maybe I'd better remind you that you do."

She pushed at his chest. "Tucker Reeves, if you kiss me now I swear you never will again!"

He grinned. "Admit you like me."

She struggled another minute before giving up. "Okay, I like you. Now let me go."

"A lot."

She tried to hide a smile. "A lot. In spite of the fact that you're a pushy, stubborn, *hairy* Neanderthal."

Tucker's eyes narrowed at the twisted compliment, but he let it go. "You taking me to dinner tonight?"

"I don't know. Jason..."

He pulled her closer. "We have an agreement, remember? Sealed with a kiss."

She rolled her eyes. "Okay, I'll take you to dinner. Now, can we go to work?"

"Yes, ma'am." Tucker released her and turned toward the dressing room. He paused at the door. "I'm not shaving."

"Look, I already gave in on the makeup..."

"I'm not shaving."

"We'll see how it looks." She retreated to her silver umbrella. "Now finish dressing."

"Please."

She glowered at him over her shoulder. "Please."

Tucker emerged from the dressing room five minutes later feeling like he'd been gussied up for his funeral. Susan had added a bolo tie with a turquoise clasp and a pure white Stetson to the satin shirt and pants.

"He's ready," Susan announced. "Where's Cassie?"

Marc pointed to a door on the other side of the studio. "Loading film."

A few minutes later Cassie came through the darkroom door, a black box in her hands. She stopped when she saw Tucker. "You're wearing that?"

Tucker flexed his muscles so the fringe along his arms danced. "You don't like the rhinestone cowboy image?"

Cassie didn't even smile. "Susan, did you pick this out?"

Susan shook her bottle-blond head emphatically. "Ms. Simmons sent it over. I thought you'd seen it."

Cassie rolled her eyes. "Why does Erica insist on helping? We're going for sexy here. Susan, do you find this sexy?"

Susan sighed dreamily. "I think Tucker would be sexy in anything."

Tucker grinned at her and Cassie frowned. "We'll try a few

shots. Then he can change. Marc, pull down the dark blue background. We'll need some contrast with this outfit."

She walked over to a sturdy black-and-chrome stand with three legs and clicked the black box onto the back of another black box. That had to be the camera, though it was bigger than any Tucker had seen. It had an accordion-sided bellows on the end and a crank on the side. She turned the crank a few times, then adjusted a few knobs with an efficiency that awed him.

"You ready?" she asked finally.

"Yes, ma'am."

She gestured toward a well-lit area where Marc had just pulled down a roll of dark blue. It covered the wall and several feet of the floor. Tucker moved to stand on it. "Now what?"

Cassie leaned over the camera, looking down through a black projection on top. "I need you to pose for me. Marc, move that flash unit on the floor in front of him. That hat's going to give us problems with shadows."

Tucker crossed his arms over his chest. "Pose."

"You know, move around. Do cowboy things."

Marc moved back to watch from beside a giant light on a heavy rolling stand. Susan stared at him from the other side of the studio. He felt like a bull in a roomful of buyers. "There aren't any cowboy things to do. Although we do stand around a lot behind the chutes. So, I am posing."

Cassie raised her head from the camera. "This is why I prefer models. Okay, we'll do it the hard way. Lift your chin a little higher and to the right. Now, put your left hand on your hip. Good."

The lights flashed.

"Now turn to the side and pull your hat a little lower. A little more. Good."

All day, through four changes of clothing, Cassie gave him explicit instructions on where to place his hands, how bright she wanted his smile, what angle to lift his chin. During their brief break for lunch Susan gave him a rope. So in the afternoon he built loops and lassoed shadows.

All in all, it was an easy way to make a buck. A helluva lot easier than riding rank bulls. And it gave him the chance to watch Cassie work, a side of her he hadn't seen before. She worked tirelessly, patiently, efficiently. She was in her element, and obviously loved her work. The speed with which her assistants carried out her instructions showed how much they respected her.

Why did it depress the hell out of him? He knew there was no future for him and Cassie. She loved her job every bit as much as he loved his. And since he lived in Colorado and she lived in New York, they had no common ground.

At some point in the afternoon, Jason showed up for a while, smirking at him from the shadows beyond the lights. If Tucker didn't know the boy was Cassie's brother, he sure wouldn't have picked him out in a crowd. Already several inches taller than Cassie, the boy had an aggressive chin and dark brown hair that kept falling across his eyes. He dressed in clothes that were three sizes too big and looked as if they'd been bought at a second-hand store.

"Okay, that's a wrap." Cassie smiled at him for the first time that day. "You were great."

Tucker didn't smile back. He gathered the rope and approached the camera. "So were you."

She held up the back of the camera she'd just removed. "We'll see about that. You can put your own clothes on now. I need to develop this film."

"Where you taking me for supper?"

Cassie stopped in midstride and looked at him over her shoulder. "I'm a little tired tonight. Why don't we just call it a day?"

In two strides he was invading her space. She looked up at him with wide eyes, but didn't back away. "Because we have an agreement, remember? Spend as much time together as possible until we're sick of each other."

Her chin raised another notch. "What if I'm already sick of you?"

"Are you?"

She looked away, but he brought her head back around with a finger under her chin. She was pushing him away, and he'd be damned before he let her. "Oh, no. You have to look me in the eye and say it."

She took a breath to speak, then released it. She searched his eyes a long minute, took another breath, then a noise behind them brought both their heads around. Marc had just raised the backdrop.

"Let's discuss this later," she said stiffly. "You can wait for me in the apartment. There's soft drinks and beer in the refrigerator. Make yourself at home."

Ten minutes later Tucker walked out of the dressing room, feeling better in his own jeans and chambray shirt. At least physically.

The studio was empty and lit now with only a single overhead light near the door to Cassie's apartment. Thirsty from long hours under the lights, he went in search of a beer.

The noise of a television hit him as soon as he opened the door. Jason lounged in front of the big screen, his feet propped on the coffee table littered with soft drink cans and candy wrappers.

Tucker didn't say anything as he walked into the kitchen. He found the beer in the refrigerator and took a long, satisfying pull. The music blaring from the TV was discordant and the singing sounded like screeching. Tucker strolled into the living room and stood directly behind Jason. Skinny, long-haired men in tight clothes and clown makeup gyrated on the screen.

"Those guys look like they could use a decent meal."

Jason sneered. "Those guys are worth millions of dollars. I think they can afford to buy food."

Tucker's eyes narrowed. "So, is this how soft city boys

spend their time? Spread out all over a couch, sucking up junk food?''

"At least we don't pretend to be John Wayne."

"That's good. John Wayne would take you by the ear and haul you out to the woodshed."

The boy rolled his eyes and turned back to the TV, dismissing Tucker. "Yeah, whatever."

Tucker studied the angry face for a long moment. It was like looking in a mirror. After spending endless years in foster homes, he'd been an older version of Jason—cocky, defensive, rude. It had taken Roy Gluck and a helluva lot of rough stock to knock some sense into him.

Maybe that's what Jason needed, someplace to vent all the frustration and to triumph for once in his life. But right now he needed to know that Tucker wasn't a threat to his relationship with his sister.

"I'm not taking Cassie away from you, Jason," Tucker said quietly. "I know you've been through hell, with your mother moving around and all, but—"

"You don't know squat about me," Jason sneered. "Shut up and go away."

Tucker leaned stiff arms on the back of the couch. "Hell, no."

Chapter Six

Tucker nearly laughed at the shocked expression on the boy's face. "You got keys to this place?"

"Duuuhhh. I live here now."

"Then get your coat. We're going shopping."

"You're crazy, man. I'm not going anywhere with you."

Tucker grabbed his sheepskin coat from a hook by the door, plus a wool army jacket that could only be Jason's. "We're going to fix supper. Your sister's worked hard all day. It's the least we can do."

"Are you deaf? I'm not going anywhere with you. Besides, I can't cook."

Tucker threw Jason's coat on top of him. "High time you learned. Get up. Unless you plan on being a tick the rest of your life."

"Tick?"

"Sucking life out of other people, giving them nothing but a bad itch."

"I can take care of myself."

Tucker stared at him. "Can you? Then prove it."

"Aw, man, you're crazy," Jason said, but rose and shrugged into his coat.

Cassie didn't realize she'd thrown two wolves together until she opened the door between the studio and apartment and heard them snarling.

"Who died and made you king?" Jason asked irritably.

"Oh, quit your belly-aching and finish. It takes a couple of hours to—"

"Oww!" was followed immediately by something clattering to the floor and rapid footsteps.

"Damn it, I told you the knife was sharp."

Knife? Cassie rounded the corner and found them in the kitchen. Tucker held Jason's wrist in what looked to Cassie like a death grip and her sharpest knife lay on the floor. Their heads shot up at her gasp and after a brief start, their expressions turned guilty. Jason's eyes were watery and red-rimmed.

"What's going on?" she demanded. "What are you doing to Jason?"

"What am I—" Tucker's eyes narrowed, and he dropped Jason's arm. "Nothing that shouldn't have been done a long time ago."

"Making my brother cry?"

"I'm not crying," Jason said indignantly.

"He's been chopping onions," Tucker said, his voice tight. "I'm teaching him how to make a decent pot of chili."

His explanation brought Cassie's indignation up short. "What?"

"Chili. You throw some ground beef, beans, tomato sauce, peppers—"

"I know what chili is." She stepped into the kitchen to take Jason's hand. "You're hurt."

"It's nothing," Jason and Tucker said in unison.

Jason pulled his hand from Cassie's grip.

"Go put a bandage on it," Tucker told him. "Then come back and finish chopping those onions."

Cassie walked out of the kitchen area with Jason. "I'll help you find—"

Jason sloughed off her arm impatiently. "I can do it."

She stood at the head of the hallway and watched him disappear into the bathroom. "The bandages are below the sink."

"I know. I saw them this morning." Jason slammed the bathroom door.

Cassie stiffened as Tucker came up behind and massaged her shoulders.

"I didn't realize chili was cruel and inhumane punishment in New York."

She walked out of his grip and into the kitchen to pick up the knife. "You surprised me, is all. I didn't know Jason knew how to cook."

"He doesn't. That's the point. A boy his age should know how to scrape a meal together. I figured there's not too many ways to mess up chili. Had to hit a couple of stores to find hot peppers, though. That's why we're running late."

She washed off the knife and stepped over to the half-cut onion. "I thought we were going out to eat."

As she began to slice, Tucker caught her wrist. He slipped the knife from her hand. "Don't finish this for him."

"Jason doesn't know how to chop onions."

"He'll never learn if you do it for him."

She stiffened, but he cut her off before she could say anything. "Don't get your hackles up, Angel. Jason's not unique. Hell, half the kids in the country have the same problem."

"And what's that, Dr. Spock?"

Either her sarcasm went over his head or he refused to acknowledge it. "Nothing's expected of them. Whoever's raising them wants to give them a better life, so they don't give their kids any chores and don't make them responsible for anything. Not even their own behavior. Give a kid something that makes him feel like he's important—that he matters—and he'll respect you more for it than if you give him a new truck."

Cassie was amazed. "How'd you get so smart about kids? You don't have any, do you?"

"No." He searched her face for a long moment.

She held her breath, knowing she was about to hear something very personal. Usually she shied away from intimate conversations with people. The less you knew about someone, the less likely they were to get involved in your life. But she wanted to hear what Tucker had to say. She wanted to know him inside out.

Finally he said, "I told you about the bunkhouse I'm gonna build."

She nodded.

"It's not for ranch hands, like you probably thought. It's for troubled boys."

"Troubled boys? You mean, like runaways?"

He nodded. "Some are. Others are just ornery. They're the kids the state has pretty much given up on."

He couldn't have surprised her more if he'd said he'd be on NASA's next mission to Mars. "Is this something you're planning, or something you already do?"

"Don't get the wrong idea. It's not me. Roy Gluck is the foreman of my ranch. He and his wife, Eileen, have been helping mixed-up kids for a long time. There's two boys at the ranch now. They want to take in more, but can't without state-approved facilities."

"Which you're going to build for them." And to get the money, Tucker was willing to risk ridicule from his peers. She'd thought he just wanted to add value to his ranch.

He nodded. "They've done so much for me."

Cassie blinked as a realization hit her. "You were one of their troubled boys, weren't you?"

Again he searched her face, then finally admitted, "Yes."

She wanted to go to him. She wanted to wrap her arms around his lean, hard body and hold on to him forever.

She clutched the edge of the counter to keep from doing it.

"My parents died in a car accident when I was seven," he

said. "Didn't have any other family to speak of. I rattled around the foster care system until I was sixteen. In nine years, I was in fourteen different foster homes."

And Cassie always thought she'd had it bad. "What happened when you were sixteen? Were you adopted?"

Tucker laughed bitterly. "Kids don't get adopted at sixteen, Cassie. Especially not ones labeled 'incorrigible.' I ran away."

Her eyes widened. "You ran away? Where did you go? What did you do?"

"I kicked around a few months, stealing food and cigarettes mostly, or stuff I could sell for food and cigarettes. Then one day the truck I hitched a ride on left me in Elbert, Colorado. I got caught stealing a pack of Twinkies cakes from the local grocery."

"Did you go to jail?"

"No, but for several months I wished it had been that easy."

"What do you mean?"

"Roy was sheriff at the time. He took me out to his ranch and put me to work. Mucking stalls, loading hay, scrubbing floors, every dirty job he could think of. I tried to run away several times, but he kept hauling me back."

"So what happened?"

"I finally realized he was more determined that I'd stay than I was to leave, so I quit trying to run. I actually began to feel useful, feel like I was doing something that may not be glamorous, but was damned important, if only to the horses. I wanted to learn more, to be a real cowboy. But Roy wouldn't teach me how to ride until I had an 'attitude adjustment.' He said I had a worse disposition than any of his cow ponies. So one day I decided to teach myself how to ride. I caught a stallion in the corral and climbed on his back." Tucker laughed at the memory.

"What's so funny?"

"I didn't know—A, that if there's any other kind of horse

available, you don't ride a stallion and—*B*, you sure as hell don't try to ride one that's not broke.''

She gasped. ''You didn't!''

He chuckled. ''I sure as hell did. That horse bucked me off so many times, I still have the bruises to prove it. Anyway, by the time Roy noticed what I was doing, I was able to stay on for a few minutes at a time. He said if I was that bull-headed, I should try my luck at some real rough stock. He took me to another ranch where they train for the rodeo. I took to it like a calf takes to its momma. Rode bareback about a year, then switched over to bulls.''

Cassie frowned. She hadn't realized how much Tucker and Jason had in common. Both had been shuffled from home to home, abused emotionally if not physically. Tucker had overcome the same things Jason would have to overcome in the next few years. Tucker knew what Jason was going through.

Here she was being a shrew about Tucker's treatment of Jason, and he was only trying to help. She cleared her throat. ''I'm sorry, Tucker. I didn't—''

The sound of the bathroom door opening cut her off.

''That's okay, Angel,'' Tucker said quietly. ''I wasn't trying to play on your sympathy. Just trying to explain where I'm coming from.''

Seconds later, Jason clomped back into the kitchen.

Tucker faced him without sympathy. ''Think you'll live?''

''No thanks to you,'' he complained. He turned to Cassie. ''Did you know he made me do everything? I've been slaving away while he lounged around drinking beer.''

Cassie arched a brow at Tucker, who grinned.

''It's starting to smell good, Jason,'' she said. ''Need some help?''

''Nah.'' He walked over to finish the onion. ''This is the only thing left to add. Unless John Wayne thinks of something else.''

''Just one more thing, Tick,'' Tucker said.

Jason groaned.

"Don't worry, you already cut these up."

"The chili peppers."

"That's right. The most important ingredient."

Tucker held up a plate of chopped peppers divided into three sections. The whiff Cassie caught burned her nose at five paces.

"Since I'm dealing with city folk here, I thought I'd give you a choice. One part and your mouth gets by with a slight tingle, but you'll be known as wimps the rest of your lives. Two parts and life begins to get interesting. Better have plenty of cold beer, plus lemonade for the kiddies. Three parts, and we've got chili. But your mouth will think a flash flood looks mighty good."

"Three," Jason said at the same time Cassie said, "One."

They grinned at each other.

"Wimp," Jason accused.

She planted her hands on her hips. "Put in three parts, and I'm ordering Chinese."

"A compromise." Tucker scraped in two parts of the peppers, stirred, then covered the pot. "Two hours to simmer and then we feast."

"Two hours?" Jason and Cassie chorused.

"I'm starving," Jason cried.

"You can't rush fine cuisine." Tucker slapped Jason's shoulder. "Now, didn't someone challenge me to a death match in Mortal Kombat?"

"Relax, Tucker. Smile. A little wider. Wider."

Tucker took a deep breath and tried to follow Cassie's instructions, but he was having a helluva time. Spending all day on the crowded streets of Manhattan—gawked at, shouted at, even whistled at—was wearing his patience thin. He felt penned in like a bull in a chute.

"Dip your head just a shade. Marc, get that light under the hat."

Tucker was jostled on either side as he pretended to walk down the sidewalk of Times Square.

"Hey, John Wayne!"

The first genuine smile he'd had in hours crept across his face as he saw Jason standing behind Cassie's shoulder. Jason had warmed up considerably after the chili episode the night before. He and Jason had formed a fragile but genuine bond while playing computer games for hours on end.

Jason was aching for attention. He desperately needed a father figure in his life—one who would stick around for more than a few years.

Tucker touched the brim of his Resistol. "Hey, Tick."

"All right," Cassie called. "I finally got a smile I can live with."

She snapped several shots, then straightened and looked around. "Marc, let's set up in front of that marquee over there. Jason, since you're here, you and Sam help Marc carry those lights. Tucker, change shirts."

Marc and Cassie began moving their equipment with the boy's help, and Susan came forward with yet another new shirt. Tucker had changed clothes more in the last three days than he had in the last month.

He yanked his snaps apart. "How long's she going to torture me?"

Susan glanced at the tiny piece of sky not blocked by tall buildings. "I'd say we have at least another hour of decent light."

He groaned and yanked off his shirt. As he bared his torso, goose bumps danced across his skin. A young man with an earring in his nose whistled.

"Pervert," Tucker mumbled.

She handed him the new shirt. "That's life in the Big Apple."

"Yeah? Well, this Big Apple has a helluva lot of worms."

Susan laughed. "Don't let it get to you."

"Hey, Tucker," Jason called as he came back across the

street. "This is Sam Evans. He wanted to meet the guy who beat me in Mortal Kombat."

Tucker stuck out his hand to the blond teenager. Sam was several inches shorter than Jason and had a soft look, though he wasn't overweight. "Beat him? Didn't he tell you he whupped my sorry butt five games to one?"

Sam looked at Tucker's hand as if uncertain what to do with it. But after a brief hesitation, he met Tucker's grip with a smile. "Yeah, but no one's ever beat him—even once. He's the best."

Tucker nodded as he snapped the new shirt. "Tick's got good instincts, all right. He'd do good on a bronc or a bull."

Sam looked at his friend in confusion. "'Tick'?"

Jason flushed, so Tucker said, "I call him that 'cause I think he'd stick to the back of a bronc like a tick."

Amazement blinked across Sam's face, and Jason smiled at Tucker gratefully. Tucker grinned back.

"Do you really ride bulls?" Sam asked.

"When they'll let me."

"Why?"

Tucker chuckled. "Why not?" He tucked in his shirt as the boys continued to ask him questions about rodeo.

Across the street, Cassie glanced around to make sure the equipment was in place. Satisfied, she started to call Tucker, but her eyes fell on the small group of males talking with animation. Even if she hadn't been looking for them, they would've drawn her attention. Tucker's white cowboy hat caught the slanted rays of the sun. His chiseled face drew her eyes like a lighthouse drew ships.

As she watched, Tucker slapped Jason on the shoulder, then kept his hand there as they talked. To her surprise, Jason didn't seem to mind. In fact, he preened under Tucker's attention.

She couldn't believe the transformation her brother had undergone in the past twenty-four hours. Tucker had spent several hours last night playing computer games with Jason. Now instead of being hostile toward Tucker, her brother came all the way uptown to introduce Sam.

So much for her theory about Jason driving Tucker away.

Tucker's hand fell from Jason's shoulder, but Jason grabbed the cowboy's sleeve and leaned close to say something. Touches. The simple act of putting a hand on another person. It looked so easy. Was that Tucker's secret? Is that how he'd won Jason over so quickly? Is that what her brother needed from her—all the hugs and kisses their mother wouldn't give him?

Cassie felt something hard drop to the pit of her stomach. Touching had never been easy for her, but if that's what it took to make her brother happy, she'd learn. After all, how hard could it be?

Ignoring the inner voice telling her exactly how hard it could be, Cassie lifted a hand and waved. "We're ready. Let's work while we've got some light."

As the late news signed off that evening, Tucker switched off the TV.

Cassie stretched like a cat beside him. The way her sweater strained across her breasts cranked his libido up several notches.

This was what he'd always dreamed life at home would be like—teasing the kid, cuddling with the wife in front of the fire or television until he could scoop her up and carry her to bed.

But he couldn't carry Cassie off to bed because Jason was in the bedroom next to hers. This wasn't his home, and it never would be. Cassie wasn't his wife, and Jason wasn't his kid.

"Guess I'd better go," he said a little harsher than he meant to.

She frowned. "Take a cab, okay?"

Tucker caught her hand. "The hotel is only four blocks away. I'll walk."

Her frown deepened. "It's freezing outside."

He stood and pulled Cassie to her feet. "Good. Maybe I won't have to take a cold shower when I get there."

Her eyes seemed to catch fire. "Tucker..."

He pulled her into his arms and his lips found hers before she could say anything else. She relaxed against him with a sigh, winding her arms around his neck and opening her mouth to his demanding tongue. His hands moved slowly down the curve of her back, pressing her closer every inch of the way. He'd barely touched her bottom when she did the work for him, grinding her hips into his.

They groaned in unison.

"Damn." He tore his lips away and pressed her head against his shoulder. "Now I'm going to have to walk a lot further than four blocks to avoid that cold shower." They both panted as if they'd run five miles. Resolutely, he turned and started toward the door. A few feet from it he stopped and said quietly, "This little plan of ours isn't working. I want you more, not less."

"I know." Her agreement was barely a whisper.

But Tucker heard it loud and clear. Wheeling around, he studied her worried face. "So, what the hell are we going to do about it?"

She released a ragged breath and frowned. "We can't stop seeing each other. We've only been shooting two days. We've still got a lot of work to do."

He raised his hand to the nape of her neck. She stiffened for an instant, then relaxed against his hand with a visible effort. Would she ever get used to his touch? The only time she didn't flinch, the only time she touched him voluntarily, was when he didn't give her time to think about it.

Suddenly it was acutely important that she reach out to him. He wanted her to trust him enough to take his hand, to touch his face, to walk into his arms. But he didn't know how to make her want to. He knew how to touch people physically, but not emotionally. He'd spent so many years scrambling from rodeo to rodeo, town to town. People came and went in the blink of an eye. He didn't have time to get to know them. It had never occurred to him to want to...until now.

He cleared the emotion from his throat. "Do you really think not seeing each other would work?"

She hesitated, then shook her head.

He relaxed in relief. "We've got to find a way to be alone. If this is just physical, it stands to reason we need to satisfy our cravings."

"Will sex cure us of each other?"

"Maybe not. But we'll both feel a helluva lot better."

She closed her eyes and ran the tip of her tongue over her lips. "Maybe."

Tucker couldn't resist the temptation. Their mouths devoured each other's until a clatter from Jason's room brought sanity flooding back.

Cassie groaned and leaned against his chest. As he held her, Tucker felt like a matchstick. If she rubbed against him once more, he'd ignite.

He pulled her around to his side and headed for the door. "I don't suppose you'd considering coming to my hotel."

She shook her head regretfully. "I can't leave Jason alone at night."

"You're right. Not in this town." He shrugged into his jacket and settled his black Resistol on his head. "What time tomorrow?"

She sighed heavily. "Ten."

"I could come an hour early..."

She shook her head sadly. "We're shooting on location again tomorrow. Marc and Susan will be here at nine to help me pack."

"Eight?"

"Jason doesn't leave for school until eight-thirty."

"Damn."

"Damn is right." She lifted a hand, stopped, and clenched it into a fist.

Tucker sucked in a quick breath. "Touch me. I won't bite."

With intense concentration, she unfurled her fingers, then slowly dragged her fingernails down the stubble along his jaw.

Tucker thought his heart might explode. He pulled her against him roughly and covered her mouth with his.

When they pulled apart long moments later, she looked up at him with her sultry cat eyes. "I thought you said you wouldn't bite."

He managed a chuckle between the deep breaths she'd reduced him to, then leaned forward and gave her one last, hard kiss. "Lock up tight."

Jason grabbed his coat from the back of the restaurant chair and stood. "You ready, Sam? It starts in twenty minutes."

Cassie glanced up in surprise. "What starts in twenty minutes?"

"The movie."

"What movie?"

Jason rolled his eyes. "The movie Sam and me are going to see. Tucker gave us the money."

"But…" She threw a questioning glance at Tucker, who dipped his head so his hat hid his smile from the boys. "You didn't ask me if it's okay. It's Wednesday, a school night and—"

"So? The movie will be over by nine o'clock. I'll do homework then."

"You don't have any tests, do you?"

"Not until Friday," Sam said before taking a last swallow of his drink.

"Is this okay with your mom?" she asked him.

"Sure. As long as someone walks me home. Tucker said he'd do it."

"Tucker did, did he?" Cassie arched a brow at the cowboy in question.

"The movie is right around the corner from my hotel," Tucker told her.

Suddenly Cassie realized that she was losing her protection.

Not protection against Tucker—protection from her own libido.

And it was about time.

They'd been working all day, but suddenly she was no longer tired. She fought the smile threatening to sweep across her face.

Without looking away from Tucker's intense blue gaze, she said, "Okay, guys. Have a good time."

As the boys left the restaurant, Cassie hesitantly reached a hand across the table. Tucker grabbed it and brought it to his lips. Her heart performed several somersaults. Touching wasn't so hard.

"You bribed them, didn't you?" she asked.

He grinned against her hand. "Hell, yes."

"I thought they had an evening of virtual killing and maiming planned."

"They did. I convinced them to change their plans. Do you mind?"

She finally gave in to the smile. "I wish I'd thought of it."

Tucker squeezed her hand and let go. "Give me five minutes to finish my steak. Have to build up my strength, you know."

"I'll get the check while you're—"

"Not tonight." He cut off another bite of meat. "Tonight it's on me."

"But Richman's paying all your expenses."

"To hell with Richman. To hell with lights and cameras and cologne. Tonight we're just a man and a woman. And where I come from, a man takes care of his woman."

Cassie sucked in a tiny breath as her heart skipped a beat. His woman. The words made her feel warm and cold at the same time. Touching was one thing, owning was something else entirely. "I'm not your woman."

His eyes roamed possessively over the parts of her body he could see above the table. "You are tonight."

She fought down the surge of desire urging her to throw

herself into his arms and say, "Take me, I'm yours." Clearing
her throat, she said, "You really are a caveman, aren't you?
And what makes it worse is, you don't even care."

"It's the cowboy way, Angel. Can't go against my raising.
And I can't help the way I feel."

Scenes from childhood restaurants flashed across Cassie's
mind. The stepfather *du jour* always paid the check, then later
expected payment of another kind from her mother. Number
Six had expected payment from Cassie, as well, though a knee
to the groin quickly discouraged him. Within a week, he'd left
them. Within six months, her mother snared Number Seven.

How was this situation different?

Suddenly she understood what drove her mother all those
years—and Cassie knew she was exactly like her. Her mother
had just wanted to be important to someone, the center of
someone's universe.

Chasing this elusive feeling led her mother to eight husbands.

Realizing what she'd almost done made Cassie feel as if
she were suffocating. She grabbed her purse and fumbled
enough money from her wallet to cover her, Jason's and Sam's
meals. "I can't do this."

Tucker froze with his fork in midair. "What's wrong?"

She threw the money on the table and shoved back her
chair. "I'm not like my mother."

"What?" His knife and fork clattered to his plate, and he
grabbed for her hand. "Where are you going?"

She avoided him by surging back to her feet. "I can't do
this, Tucker. This is not who I am."

"But..."

Before he could say anything that would make her change
her mind, she turned and bolted out the restaurant door.

Chapter Seven

Tucker watched Cassie scurry out, feeling as dazed and confused as he did when a bull's hoof clipped his head. Her mother? What the hell did his paying for supper have to do with her mother?

By the time he'd called the waiter over and covered the remaining portion of the bill, Cassie was gone. He knew only one place to look and twenty minutes later, he was pressing the buzzer at her building. He got no response.

He buzzed for five minutes and was just about to give up when the intercom told him, "Go away."

He smiled grimly and pushed the intercom button. "Hell, no."

"Tucker, I'm not in the mood."

"I don't care what kind of mood you're in, Angel. I deserve an explanation and I intend to get it. I'm laying on this buzzer until you let me in."

There was a brief hesitation before the door buzzed and the intercom said, "Damn you."

When he reached her door, he knocked loudly.

Several locks clicked, then the door opened the space of the chain lock. One green eye peered out. "What do you want?"

"Open the door."

"Why?"

Tucker crossed his arms over his chest. "I'm not saying a word until you let me in."

Cassie muttered words he couldn't understand, then closed the door, slid off the chain and opened it wide. "Did anyone ever tell you you're the most stubborn man on the face of the earth?"

He strode in. "Being stubborn is my profession. If a cowboy's not stubborn, he sure can't stick to the back of a bull."

She slammed the door behind him. "Well, I've just discovered your first undesirable trait, haven't I? No, wait a minute. Chauvinism was the first one. We're racking up quite a list here."

He stopped in the middle of the huge living space, his eyes narrow. "You're a feminist?"

Her chin lifted. "Not a feminist. An independentist."

"A what?"

She crossed her arms over her stomach. "I believe that everyone—man or woman—should take care of themselves. I don't need a big strong man waltzing into my life and taking over. I don't want anyone paying for my meals, telling me what to wear, and ordering me around."

"What the hell are you talking about?"

She inhaled a breath to reply, then closed her eyes and released it all at once. "Oh, never mind."

He took a step toward her, but cut it short when she flinched. "Have I ever told you what to wear? Have I ever ordered you to do anything? Hell, you're the one ordering me around. 'Smile, Tucker.' 'Lift your chin, Tucker.'"

"That's not the same thing and you know it."

He threw his arms in the air. "I don't know anything. You're confusing the hell out of me. All I wanted to do was buy your supper."

"That's how it starts, with the small things."

"How what starts?"

"The dependence. Don't you see? I refuse to be like my mother."

"What the hell does your mother have to do with this?"

Cassie opened her mouth to say something, then closed it. She searched his face for a moment, then wheeled away.

He caught her arm. "What could be so bad that you can't tell me? If you don't let me get to know you, how the hell am I going to get sick of you?"

"It's just... I've never been one to talk about myself."

"I told you my story. Don't you think it's fair you tell me yours?"

She looked at him as if she hated him, then yanked her arm from his grasp. "It was men, okay? My mother has been married eight times. When one guy left, she found another. Within six months, usually. A year at most."

"Is that all? The way you were acting, I thought she was on Wanted posters everywhere."

"I never said it was anything major. I'm just not real proud of it. She married Number Eight a couple of months ago. He's as much a jerk as the rest of them. That's why Jason is going to live with me for a while."

"Okay." Tucker pushed back the brim of his hat. "But I still don't see what this has to do with me buying you supper."

"Don't you understand? Mother can't do anything for herself. She needs a man for everything. Her husbands pay her bills, they feed her children, they control every aspect of her life. She can't do the simplest things for herself. And just when she starts depending on them, they leave."

"What about your own father? Why didn't you live with him?"

"He died in a hunting accident when I was three. I don't remember him."

Tucker reached for her hand and was surprised when she

let him take it. "I know what having so many fathers is like. Did any of them…treat you bad?"

"One tried. Once. I got away from him." She took an uneven breath, her eyes far away. "Most of them couldn't care less whether I was around or not. All except Jason's father. Mr. Warner bought me my first camera. But he died, too. A heart attack."

Tucker studied Cassie's tight face. This was his first real glimpse inside Cassie. He felt as if he'd just been handed a present. He wanted to give her something back, to say something profound, something to heal this sore on her psyche. But he was no psychiatrist. "I've known women like your mother, and you're not like them. With most of them, it's not that they can't do things for themselves, they just won't. There's a big difference."

Cassie considered his point, then shook her head. "Maybe. But whether it's laziness or ineptitude, the result is the same. She has sold her life to a man eight times. I'm never going to do that."

"No one's asking you to," he said quietly. "I'm not trying to control you, or take over your life. I'm just asking for a small piece of it. In exchange, I'll give you a piece of mine."

"But what you said at the restaurant…"

"I'm sorry if I scared you. I'm not used to independent women. Most of the ones I come across assume the man pays for the meal—and everything else. That's pretty much how it works all the way 'round in my neck of the woods. It's the way I was raised."

Her solemn, green eyes searched his face, and Tucker wondered if she was thinking the same thing he was. A cowboy and an independent woman mixed about as well as oil and water. They were much further apart than the miles separating their homes. Their differences went soul deep.

Though they'd been doomed from the beginning, he saw it for the first time with crystal clarity.

Who needs you?

He'd never felt so alone in his life.

When she finally spoke, her words echoed his thoughts. "This is never going to work."

"No." He rubbed a finger across the back of her hand. "But we've known that from day one."

"So why do I still want you?"

Fire flashed through him, followed quickly by a flare of hope. Every muscle in his body clenched to keep him from grabbing her and throwing her on the nearest couch. "We all want what we can't have. It's human nature."

She swallowed convulsively. "It contradicts every rule I've made for my life, but I can't help it."

Moving slowly so he wouldn't spook her, he lifted his other hand and smoothed back a wisp of hair that had escaped her braid. "So what do you suggest we do about it?"

Closing her eyes, she took in a jerky breath. "I suppose nothing has really changed, has it?"

He stepped close and slipped his arm around her waist, pulling her body against his. "No."

With a sad sigh, she rested her head against his chest. "We're just racking up reasons that will help us cope when you leave."

"Is that what we're doing?"

She arched her neck and looked at him, regret shadowing her green eyes. "It's what we better be doing."

Knowing she was right but unable to agree, he lowered his head by degrees. "All I know is now. All I want to think about is now. For now, just let me make love to you. Let's leave tomorrow for tomorrow."

As she breathed his name, his lips touched hers. His first kiss was tentative, gently persuasive, but Cassie would have none of that. She opened her mouth and ran her tongue across his teeth. Tucker needed no further enticement. His tongue dipped into her mouth, plunging into every soft crevice.

She whimpered, and her hands swept up his back. She knocked off his hat and plunged both hands into his hair, pulling his lips even harder against hers. That left her body free for his hands to roam, and he took full advantage. Tightening his hold around her waist, his free hand tested the weight of one breast. Her moan drifted into every pore of his body, bathing him with heat.

Suddenly she pulled away. As she stared at him he held his breath, trying to keep from swearing. But instead of ending their love play, she took his hand and led him down the hall to her bedroom.

The door closed behind them with a satisfying click, and he pulled her into his arms. "Finally."

They kissed their way to the canopied bed where Tucker scooped Cassie up and laid her across the thick flowered comforter. Heart racing like a stampeding herd, he shucked his boots, tossed aside his shirt, and joined her.

She purred like a cat as she splayed her fingers across his chest. He let her hands roam while he unwound her hair from its braid. He combed through the silk with his fingers, spreading the fiery strands across the pillow. "It's so…"

"Red?" she supplied with a wry smile.

He grinned. "Well, yeah, it's definitely red. But it's beautiful, and sexy…like you."

Her cat's eyes softened, and she pulled his lips to hers.

As he savored her taste and textures, he deftly unbuttoned her shirt. When he pushed it off, she twisted a hand to her back to unhook her bra. She lifted her arms to slide it off, and his mouth fell on the bounty exposed. She sucked in a quick breath and arched her back, silently begging for his touch.

Heat burned through him as his tongue wrapped around the tip of one breast, then the other. Her pink areolae darkened and tightened into pebbly buds that scraped across his tongue.

"Damn," he growled. "You taste better than a thirty-dollar steak."

Her chuckle was broken off by a gasp as he took one breast into his mouth. She flexed beneath him and raked her nails across his shoulders.

He could feel Cassie's heart as it pounded liquid fire through the delicate veins. He could hear her harsh, uneven breathing.

Suddenly there were too many clothes between them. Lifting himself away, he fumbled with the belt of her pants. She understood immediately. Her hands fell to her waist and a minute later he only had her French-cut, red silk panties to deal with.

He'd just slipped a finger under the elastic when the distant sound of laughter brought his head up. They froze, listening. They could clearly hear boys talking, then the door to the apartment closed.

"Cassie?" Jason called. "You here?"

Cassie groaned. "This can't be happening."

"Damn," Tucker muttered. He scooted down on the bed and grabbed his boots. "Damn, damn, damn, damn, damn."

Cassie rose to her knees and rapidly gathered her scattered clothes. "The movie can't be over yet. What are we going to do?"

"If we're quiet, maybe they'll think we aren't here. Will Jason check your room?"

"I don't know. He might. Did we lock the door?"

"Look," they heard Sam say. "Isn't this Tucker's hat?"

"So much for that plan," Tucker whispered as Cassie groaned again.

"Yeah," Jason replied. "What's it doing on the floor? Tucker? Cassie?"

"Maybe they're in the darkroom."

They heard the door to the studio open and close.

"Now." Tucker surged to his feet and grabbed his shirt. "I'll stall them while you get dressed."

He opened the door, cursing when he realized it was unlocked. He couldn't hear the boys in the studio, but that meant they couldn't hear him, either. He stepped into the bathroom by the kitchen and flushed the toilet.

The door to the studio opened seconds later.

Sam entered in with Jason close behind. Seeing Tucker standing in the hall, Sam stopped. "Oh. Hi."

Jason pushed Sam all the way in and closed the door. "You're here? Didn't you hear us call?"

"I was…" He pointed to the bathroom where the toilet was still running.

"Oh. Where's Cassie?"

Tucker glanced at her bedroom door. "She spilled something on her shirt. She's changing."

"Okay. Good. Now we can play on the computer."

"What are you doing home?" Tucker asked. "The movie shouldn't be over for another hour at least."

"It was sold out," Sam said.

"On a school night?" Cassie called, drawing all eyes as she opened the bedroom door and walked down the hall to join them.

Tucker winced when he saw she had on the same shirt. Their aborted lovemaking had painted her cheeks a deep crimson, but at least she'd rebraided her hair.

"Yeah," Jason told her with obvious disgust. "Can you believe it? But it just started last weekend and everybody wants to see it."

"Oh. That's too bad."

Tucker saw the sincerity of her statement as her gaze met his. Apparently the boys didn't notice Cassie's face or clothes. Thank God for the obliviousness of teenagers.

"Turn the computer on," Jason told Sam. "I'll grab some snacks."

As Jason passed, he asked, "You're going to play, aren't you, Tucker?"

"I'll be there directly," he replied.

When the boys disappeared into their separate corners, Tucker pulled Cassie into his arms for a quick kiss. "We're never going to be alone."

"Tucker?" Jason called from the kitchen. "You want a beer?"

"No, get me a soda," Tucker told him, then he lowered his voice so only Cassie could hear. "If my inhibitions are loosened a single shred, I'll grab you and carry you off to my lair."

Cassie sighed with frustration. "Are you sure you want to spend another evening playing computer games?"

"I don't mind."

Cassie searched his eyes with a half-dazed, half-confused expression.

"What?" he demanded.

She ran her fingernails lightly down the stubble on his cheek. "You're a good man, Tucker Reeves. Sam and Jason ruined your..."

"Sex life?" he supplied with a grin.

She smiled. "And you don't take it out on them. In fact, you reward them by playing with them."

He shrugged. "They don't know they ruined anything."

"I know. Still..." She glanced down, then back up. "Thank you."

"For what?"

"For helping Jason. For helping me."

He shrugged. "It's noth—"

"No," she said quickly. "It isn't nothing. At least, not to me."

He studied her earnest face. Since he knew how much it cost her to admit dependence of any kind, her words had even more meaning. "You're welcome, Angel."

She smiled and since they'd reached the office where the computer was kept, she kissed him softly and pulled away.

As he watched her disappear into the darkroom, he was struck with a realization so profound, his mind reeled with the implications.

Cassie needed him.

Tucker smiled. At last he'd found a woman who needed something he had to offer.

"Tucker?"

"Coming, Tick." Tucker turned into the office, but glanced over his shoulder before stepping in.

Oil and water could be mixed, but it took a helluva lot of shaking.

There were only two problems as far as he could see—making Cassie realize she needed him, then making her admit it.

Several hours later, Cassie crossed her arms on the light table and let her head drop on top of them.

She had to face the truth. She couldn't take a decent photograph of Tucker.

Was she too close to the subject? Did wanting him make her incapable of capturing his essence on film? That defied all logic. The sexual tension between them should be heightening her instincts, letting her capture the intimacy she craved every minute of the day, both waking and sleeping.

"Cassie? You okay?"

Her head shot up at the quiet question. Tucker stood at the door to the darkroom, his coat slung over his shoulder.

"Yes. No. I don't know." She rubbed her aching temples. "I'm beginning to think I'm never going to be okay again."

He threw his coat on a counter and strode across the room. His big, strong hands rubbed her shoulders. "What's wrong?"

"Mmm. That feels good." Cassie rolled her head forward as he massaged. "It's the photos I've been taking. They aren't any good."

His hands paused. "Does this mean I have to give back all the money? I've already given the contractor the go-ahead on the bunkhouse and—"

"No," she said quickly. "It means... I don't know what it means. It's not your fault. It's mine."

"Hey, Tucker!" Jason called. "You ready to walk Sam home?"

"In a minute," Tucker called back, then he leaned over her. "Are these the pictures? Can I see them?"

She waved her hand over the transparencies. "Look all you want."

He moved to her side and bent over the light table.

"What's going on?" Jason asked from the doorway. Sam stood behind him.

Cassie was about to say, "Nothing," but Tucker waved the boys over.

"Come here and look at these pictures."

"What are they?" Jason asked as they approached the light table.

"Tucker," Cassie said as she slipped off the stool to make room.

"Cool," Sam said.

The three male heads bent over the light table.

"These are real good, Cassie," Sam said in a polite voice.

"No, they're not." Jason glanced over his shoulder. "They look fake."

Cassie was amazed at his perception. "You're right. I just don't know why."

Tucker leaned his hip against the light table. "I know."

Her eyes widened. "You do?"

"I'm not a photographer or anything…"

"Tell me," she pleaded. "I'm desperate for suggestions."

"How can they look real with city backgrounds? You're wanting a cowboy to sell this smelly stuff, but a cowboy who's not around cows or horses looks about as at home as a lion pacing back and forth in a zoo cage."

Cassie stared at him a second, then went to her filing cabinet and pulled out the photos she'd taken of him at the rodeo. She spread them on the light table and the three males gathered close.

"Wow, Cassie. These really *are* good," Sam said.

Tucker had hit the proverbial nail on the head. The shots in the studio looked as fake as the fake backgrounds. The city shots were even worse.

Why hadn't she been able to see that?

She knew why. This was the first time that the concept she'd come up with for photographs was all wrong. There'd been times when she'd been a little off, but minor adjustments fixed those problems. This required a whole new perspective.

A new concept took shape as she compared the two sets of photographs. But the fact that she had to come up with another one felt like a kick in the pants. It was a reminder that she hadn't been keeping her mind on business.

"You're absolutely right, Tucker," she said softly. "The backgrounds are the difference. We'll have to go on location, assuming Mr. Richman okays the expense. But I'm sure Erica can talk him into it. Any rodeos in March?"

"There's rodeos all year 'round." Tucker squinted as he remembered the doctor's advice about quitting rodeo. He couldn't take it before because he'd needed the money for the new bunkhouse and riding bulls was the only way to get it. Since he'd found out how much he'd make posing for this cologne, he'd actually been considering taking the doctor's advice. Now he'd have to ride at least one more time.

But he wasn't worried. He'd ridden hundreds of times without getting hurt. Though injuries were part of rodeo, they certainly didn't happen every time a cowboy got on the back of a bucking animal.

So Tucker shoved the doctor's advice into a corner of his mind.

Pushing his hat back, he tried to remember the list of rodeos listed in the *Prorodeo Sports News*. "Off the top of my head, I know of two this weekend—Austin and Phoenix."

"Which do you think would be better?" she asked.

He rubbed his chin. "Well, I've already paid the entry fee for Phoenix. I won't be able to ride in the actual rodeo in Austin. But if Austin's better for you, we can rig something up."

She shook her head. "Doesn't make any difference to me. One's as good as the other. Will they let me get close enough to shoot?"

Tucker grinned. "Yep, Phoenix'll be better. I know the promoter there. He'll let you on the arena floor to shoot pictures if I ask just right. I'd better call tonight, though."

Cassie pointed to the phone. "Call him now. Do you know the number? We'll have to hustle if we're going to be ready to leave tomorrow."

"I'll have to call someone else to get the number," Tucker said as he headed for the phone. "But what about Jason?"

Cassie turned to Sam. "Think it'll be okay with your mother if Jason stays with y'all for a few days?"

Sam shrugged. "Sure. We're not going anywhere."

"Call her, please. You can use the phone after Tucker."

"But I want to go with you," Jason told her. "I can miss a day of school. It's spring break next week and we won't be doing anything."

"There's that algebra test tomor—"

Jason shoved Sam's shoulder to cut him off.

Cassie frowned at her brother. "No, Jason. You're too new at this school to miss a test."

Tucker paused with his hand on the receiver as an idea hit him. "Jason, why don't you fly out to Denver on Sunday? We'll pick you up and you can spend spring break at my ranch."

Cassie frowned. "Your ranch?"

He nodded, hoping she wouldn't see how important this sudden idea was to him. He wanted to show her his world, and though he knew the possibility was remote, he wanted to see how she fit into that world. At the very least, they'd have another week together. "You can take pictures there, too. A ranch is even more real than a rodeo."

"Please, Cassie?" Jason begged.

"Tell you what," she told him. "You make at least a B on that algebra test, and it's a deal."

He made a pained face, then straightened his shoulders. "Okay, I will."

Cassie's gaze locked into Tucker's as the boys discussed

the trip's possibilities. Her green eyes shone with such promise that he suddenly realized they'd be alone at the Phoenix hotel.

Tucker smiled as warmth spread into body parts that had no business getting hot, not with two kids in the room. To hide his reaction, he turned back to the counter and began pushing buttons on the phone.

Chapter Eight

"**Y**ou did what?"

Tucker glanced up from packing film into his duffel bag to see Cassie clutching the phone with an incredulous look. He pushed his hat back. Whatever had happened, he hoped it wouldn't keep them from leaving.

She sighed heavily. "Well, it can't be helped now, can it? Do you know if Zach is free? ...Oh, he's working for Gregor this week. Pete? Julio? ...Oh, well, I'll find somebody. You take care of yourself. 'Bye."

She hung up the phone and groaned. "Great. Just great."

Tucker rose to his feet. "What happened?"

"Marc slipped a disc riding a mechanical bull at Spurs and Suds last night." Her eyes narrowed. "He said he got the idea from you."

"Me? All I did was answer questions about rodeo. I didn't know he'd do something loco."

Cassie rubbed the bridge of her nose. "I know. Marc tends to be a little reckless. But the plane leaves in two hours. We've got to be on it if we're going to make the rodeo. Where am I going to find another assistant?"

Tucker walked over and began massaging her shoulders. He planned on getting rid of her tension in a much more pleasurable way that night. They'd already discussed sharing a room at the hotel where they could hang a Do Not Disturb sign on the door and tell the operator to hold their calls. He'd be climbing into bed with a helluva lot more relish than he'd be climbing on the back of a bull. "Do you really need an assistant?"

She rolled her head to the side, stretching the muscles of her neck under his probing fingers. "I've never been on a shoot without at least one."

"You didn't have any assistants in Florida."

"They'd already gone home. I stayed a day extra to shoot the rodeo."

"What about Susan?"

Cassie shook her head. "She's makeup and wardrobe only."

"We can handle things between the two of us, can't we?"

Her gaze drifted away as she considered his question. "Well, I suppose. The worst part will be hauling all that equipment around. But I could make do with the bare essentials. If I absolutely have to have something I've left behind, I can always rent it in Phoenix."

He pulled her arms around his waist, tugging her against him. "If we don't have an assistant tagging along, we've got that much more time alone."

Cassie's eyes dropped to his lips. "You've convinced me."

A familiar warmth stole through him, one he knew he'd remember long after Cassie left him. But he didn't want to consider there might be a time when they wouldn't be together. He wanted to enjoy the now.

He dipped his head slowly and felt his voice deepen. "Want a preview of tonight's performance?"

Her smile was sultry. "On the bull?"

"Angel, you can create any fantasies you want."

Her chuckle turned to a moan as his lips touched hers. He

splayed his hands across her back and pulled her tighter as his mouth plundered hers.

"Tucker?" she said between kisses.

"Hmm?"

"We've got to pack..." Another kiss. "...the equipment..." Another kiss. "...and get to the airport."

"Damn." He kissed her again—hard—and released her. "Then you'll just have to wait."

She turned toward the studio. "Damn."

Tucker slipped down gingerly onto Jawbreaker's back, keeping his boots planted high on the rails. This bull was a "chute fighter," just one of the tactics the beefy Charolais used to psyche out the cowboy about to ride him.

As longtime friend, Bud Kimbro, reached underneath the bull's belly to catch the tail of the bull rope, he kept up a litany of instructions on how to ride the bull. Tucker listened with only half an ear.

The main reason Jawbreaker was hard to ride was that he followed no set pattern. Most bulls had a routine, which bull riders remembered—spinning to the left or to the right, bucking straight out and then spinning, whatever. This routine was known as the bull's "book." But Jawbreaker's book changed plots every time he left the chute.

Tucker knew anticipation would do him in. Success depended on instinct alone. He had to turn off his brain and simply react—staying with the bull move for move, jump for jump, kick for kick.

He closed his eyes for a couple of seconds. A familiar calm settled over him like a quiet fog. He slid his hand, palm up, into the flat-braided loop on the bull rope. Bud pulled it tight. Tucker nodded and took the tail of the rope. He wound it around his hand, gave it a twist, then laid the tail forward of the handhold. With his left hand, he pounded down the fingers of his resined glove.

The arena director laced the jerk rope through the chute

gate. Tucker screwed his hat onto his head and scooted up on his hand. The doctor's advice flitted across his mind, but he forced it away.

Fear of injury was a self-fulfilling prophecy.

Jawbreaker took a deep breath and snorted, tightening the bull rope against Tucker's gloved hand. The movement felt so familiar that Tucker smiled. This was where he belonged. It was what he'd been born to do.

Taking his own deep breath, Tucker nodded.

Cassie stood in the loose dirt of the Phoenix arena, doing a last-minute check on the cameras hanging around her neck. Tucker had secured permission for her to shoot from the arena floor, with strict instructions for her to run if a bull even glanced in her direction.

Being only yards away from the action was a far better spot than sitting on the fence. Even so, she'd only have eight seconds to get a decent shot of Tucker on the back of this bull— if they were both lucky. A shiver ran down her spine as she remembered Tucker's ride in Florida.

"Howdy, ma'am."

She looked up to see one of the two bull fighters standing next to her. He had the makeup and dress of a clown, but wore athletic shoes instead of big feet. A bull fighter's job was to distract the bull after the cowboy dismounted, and his only defense was running.

Cassie smiled and asked over the noise of the crowd, "You're Leech McGarren, aren't you? Tucker told me to look for your purple hat. I'm Cassie Burch. You were at the only other rodeo I've attended—in Kissimmee, Florida."

"I remember. You're the lady Tucker knocked off the fence." He lifted his hat and scratched sandy hair. "I ain't real proud of that night. That's one bull that got clean away from me. Ol' Crazy Eight's a mean one."

"What about Jawbreaker?" she asked, unable to conceal her worry about the bull Tucker had to ride.

"Oh, Jawbreaker ain't mean, even though he ain't never been rode."

Her heart skittered past a beat. "What do you mean, never been rode?"

"Nobody's made the buzzer on him. Shucks cowboys off quicker'n a wink and heads for the gate. But he don't go after 'em with murder on his mind."

She relaxed a fraction. "Then Tucker can't be hurt."

"Didn't say that. There's all kinds of ways of gettin' hurt besides being gored—gettin' stomped on, plowed into the fence, or just hittin' the dirt wrong."

Cassie felt blood rush from her face.

Leech must've noticed because he winced. "Shucks, I didn't mean to worry you none. Tucker's gonna do just fine. I'm gonna stick close as a calf to its momma, and help him all I can. Figger I owe him."

Cassie swallowed hard and tried to smile, but Leech's assurance didn't relieve her mind. "Thanks. I'd appreciate all the help you can give him."

He nodded and looked at the chute where Tucker was preparing to ride. "Truth tell, I'm kinda surprised to see him here. But hell, he never did follow a doctor's orders. What cowboy does?"

Cassie froze. "Doctor's orders?"

"Doc told him to quit riding on account of that concussion he got at Kissimmee. Told him if he got another bonk on the head he'd—" Leech cut his words off abruptly as his eyes returned to Cassie's bloodless face.

She grabbed the bull fighter's arm and demanded, "He'd what?"

"Aw, hell, you was there. I thought you knew."

"Knew what?" She shook his sleeve so hard it ripped. "Tell me."

Leech screwed his hat down onto his head. "Uh, looks like Tucker's about to give the nod."

"Wait! You've got to stop him."

The bull fighter shook his head. "Tucker ain't never drawed out, ma'am. I don't imagine he's about to start. 'Scuse me. I've got to earn my paycheck."

He shrugged off her hand and sprinted to the other side of the chute. Cassie's eyes flew to chute number four. Tucker was hidden by a row of cowboys hanging over the gate. As if preparing for the violence to come, Jawbreaker slammed against the gate of the chute. Cowboys scattered like newspapers in a strong wind.

"Tucker, no," she whispered, frozen in shock. But the thought of never seeing her cowboy again galvanized her. She sprinted for the gate, shouting, "Tucker, stop!"

She hadn't taken two strides when he nodded. A cowboy grabbed her around the waist as the gate swung open.

"Tucker!"

Jawbreaker exploded through the gate as it swung open, slamming Tucker's right knee into the post. Pain shot up his leg. The bull spun to the left, throwing Tucker's leg farther back on his right side and off his rope. Tucker pulled himself back by brute strength, only to be slung around to the right.

Tucker kept his eyes glued to the bull's head. The hulking bands of muscles beneath the rolling skin stretched and flexed between Tucker's legs as Jawbreaker tried every trick known by bulls to throw him off. Every spin threw Tucker off balance, but every time he jerked himself back into the well.

As Tucker's hat flew in the air, Jawbreaker bellowed in anger and changed tactics. Planting his front feet on the ground, he kicked his heels high into the air. Tucker felt himself slip an inch further onto his hand.

The buzzer blew, but Tucker didn't celebrate. Jawbreaker wasn't finished with him. On the second jump, the monster's back came up so high, it slammed Tucker over and off. He somersaulted over the bull's left shoulder. But his hand didn't come free.

He was hung up.

Jawbreaker continued to kick, bouncing Tucker around like a rag doll. Leech and his bull-fighting partner tried to join the fray, but Jawbreaker wouldn't let them close.

Desperately, Tucker tried to grab the tail of the bull rope but it kept flopping away. On the second buck, the momentum threw him back and Tucker felt his arm wrench out of its shoulder socket. Pain knifed through him.

A second later Leech appeared across the withers, jerking on the tail of the rope. The other clown slapped the bull on the muzzle to distract him.

Finally the rope gave way. Tucker fell flat on his back in the dirt. As the crowd screamed, pain swirled with the arena lights above him, then pinpointed in and out of sight.

Before the gate closed on the retreating bull, Cassie slammed her foot down onto her captor's boot and ran. She was the first to kneel at Tucker's side. His face was white as bleached cotton, his form still as death.

"Tucker, look at me," she yelled. She heard herself clearly in the sudden hush of the crowd. "Wake up!"

She wanted to slap his face to bring him around, but didn't dare. What if he'd injured his head again?

Half a second later, they were surrounded by cowboys.

"What's the matter with him?"

"Passed out."

"Look how his arm's twisted."

"Hell, he done wrenched it. Good thing he's out cold."

The words spoken above her brought Cassie's attention to Tucker's right shoulder. It bulged unnaturally, and his arm lay twisted at an odd angle, half underneath his body.

"Somebody help him," she pleaded.

"The Justin Healers are on their way, ma'am," an older man said.

Tucker's eyes fluttered open, then immediately shut tight as he winced.

"Tucker, can you hear me?" Cassie cried.

He nodded slightly. Sweat popped out all over his face.

"You in pain, Tuck?" the older man asked.

"I've been...better," he groaned.

"The doctor's here. Ma'am, you've got to move outta his way."

Cassie protested as strong hands lifted her away. "He needs me."

"He needs these guys worse." The familiar voice drew her head around. Leech's face was grim under his makeup. "They'll help him, Cassie. Don't worry. This is why they're here. They do this all the time."

They laid a stretcher out a few feet away from Tucker, then kneeled beside him, blocking her view. She swallowed hard at the realization that this is what Tucker faced every day he got on the back of a bull, what all bull riders faced. "I think they're all a bunch of idiots."

"The Justin Healers?" Leech asked in confusion.

She shook her head so hard her braid whipped around. "Bull riders. And Tucker's the biggest idiot of all."

"It's just a separated shoulder. He could'a got hung up on any bull in the pen back there."

"Like I said, they're all id—"

"Sh—"

The loud curse, bitten off, drew her attention back to Tucker. A step to the right let her catch a glimpse of his face between two burly cowboys. He was no longer conscious. The men with the Justin logo on their backs rose and several cowboys helped them lift Tucker onto the stretcher. His shoulder no longer bulged, and they'd taped his arm flat against his side.

Cassie followed the stretcher out of the arena as the spectators rose to their feet, clapping wildly. Leech stayed close behind her. The ambulance that stayed parked at the gate during performances was already running and the cowboys pushed Tucker's stretcher on top of the gurney.

"I'm going with him," Cassie declared to the paramedics.

"You related?"

Her eyes widened. They wouldn't let her go with him unless she was related? One glance at Tucker's still form, and Cassie was ready to lie.

Before she could, Leech was shoving her past the paramedics, into the ambulance. "Tonight she is."

Cassie pulled down the tiny seat and looked at Leech. "Thanks."

He nodded and stepped back so they could close the doors. The vehicle inched forward.

"Strap in," the attendant told her.

As Cassie tugged the seat straps around her, her hand struck the zoom lens on one of the four cameras still hanging around her neck. She glanced down in surprise. She was so accustomed to their weight, she'd forgotten all about the—

Cassie closed her eyes and groaned.

After all Tucker went through, she hadn't taken a single picture.

Cassie shifted on the molded-plastic seat in the emergency room waiting area, trying to keep her butt from going numb.

She glanced at the clock, but the minute hand had only moved three notches since she'd last looked. What were they doing to him? She'd get up and pace if she didn't have to haul four heavy cameras with her.

The shrill scream of a child in the row behind startled Cassie, drawing her attention to the crowded room.

So many people—and she'd never felt so alone.

Ever since she'd watched Tucker being wheeled through those swinging double doors, she'd sat in numb silence, unable to think past the pain of almost losing him. Never with any other human being had she experienced such wrenching anguish as she did when he'd fallen to the dirt. It was as if her heart had been ripped from her chest.

Why did she feel this way? She didn't love the man, she just wanted him.

So why did the thought of losing him make her so crazy she forgot to do her job? That had never happened before. Never.

But then, she'd never been the focus of so much sexual and emotional attention before. Tucker satisfied some stupid need in her to be needed, to be the center of someone's universe. No one had ever made her feel this way. It scared her more than walking alone at night through Central Park.

Ever since he swaggered into her life, her emotions had been on the roller coaster from hell. And she didn't like it one single bit. She didn't like his needing her. She didn't like needing him to need her. It meant he was special. It meant she was in danger of falling in love.

No!

She was *not* in love with him. She refused to love him. She refused to love any man—except Jason.

So she wanted Tucker's body? That was just sex.

So she craved his smile. So the timbre of his deep voice sent shivers down her spine. So she needed to touch him constantly when he was near. Sex, sex, sex. That's all it boiled down to.

That's all it was now, and that's all it would ever be.

"Cassie Burch?"

Her thoughts scattered and her head jerked up. "Yes?"

The nurse's gaze zeroed in on her. "Please come with me."

Cassie threaded an arm through the camera straps and rose. "Is Tucker okay?"

The nurse nodded and held open one of the double doors. "Turns out it was only a partial dislocation, but they've admitted him so they can do some tests in the morning. Dr. Brown wants to make certain he hasn't torn the rotator cuff."

Cassie had no idea what that meant, so she plied the nurse with questions as they twisted and turned their way up to Tucker's room. By the time the nurse pushed open the door, Cassie's own shoulder throbbed.

She entered the room and found him sitting up against the raised bed, his chest bare, his face tight with pain.

She wanted to rush to him and gather him close, to assure herself that he was still alive. She wanted to pummel him until he promised never to even think about a bull again. Instead, she marched to the end of the bed and crossed her arms over her chest.

"Aw, Angel, don't start in on me. I'm hurtin' enough." Then his face brightened with a grin. "But I rode that son of a gun. Didn't happen to catch my score, did you?"

"Your score?" She threw her arms in the air, and the cameras bounced against her side. "You were almost killed, and you're worried about a score?"

He shook his head. "I'm not worried about it. It's got to be in the high eighties, at least, or those judges are as crooked as a snake in a cactus patch."

Cassie took in air to reply, then released it in a huff. "I give up." She slipped the heavy cameras off her shoulder and laid them across the empty bed. "You're actually proud of yourself, aren't you?"

"I rode him, Cassie. Nobody's lasted eight seconds on that son of a wall-eyed cow, 'cept me. It's like you shooting a picture that wins...what's the biggest prize you can win?"

"The Pulitzer?"

"Yeah, that. Cowboys all over the country—hell, all over the world'll be talking about it. Whenever ol' Jawbreaker slides into a chute, a bull rider'll turn to another and say, 'Only one cowboy's ever rode that bull—Tucker Reeves.'"

"Is it better than winning the National Finals?"

He stroked his chin with the hand of his uninjured left arm. "Purt' near."

"Is it worth giving up sex for who knows how long?" She nodded at the horrified look on his face. "So *now* you remember the night of lovemaking you promised me. How long's it going to be before we get another chance, Tucker? Who knows if we'll ever have the chance? I can't shoot pictures of you in this condition, and I can't just kill time until you get well.''

He leaned forward and grabbed her hand, though his face went white with the effort. Concerned by his pain, she let him pull her down onto the edge of the bed and gave him a moment to let it pass.

"I'll be all right in a couple of days," he said in a rough voice.

She shook her head. "Not if it's a torn rotator cuff. The nurse said six weeks and a lot of physical therapy."

"It's not a torn cuff."

"You won't know that until the doctor does those tests in the morning."

He nodded. "Angel, when you've been in this business as long as I have, you know exactly how each injury feels. This wasn't even a fully dislocated shoulder. It'll be sore for a few days, but I'll work through it. You can take a couple of days' vacation—can't you?—and wait while I—"

Cassie tensed. "You're not going to get on the back of another bull. I absolutely forbid it."

Tucker leaned back against the pillows and searched her face. How many times had he overheard similar conversations between other bull riders and their wives? How many times had he wished someone gave a damn whether he survived his next bull ride? Did Cassie care more than she'd admit? Pleasure drenched him like a warm summer rain at the possibility. "You plannin' on sticking around and enforcing that rule?"

Frustration swept over her face. "You can't mean to ride another bull tomorrow! You're hurt, Tucker. You have to mend."

Tucker sighed. What had he expected, that she'd fall all over him and beg to stay with him forever? He'd already discovered that forever wasn't high on her list of priorities. "No, I'm not going to ride a bull tomorrow. By working through it I meant I'd use my shoulder normally. Getting my picture taken won't put a lot of stress on it. I thought we'd head on back to the Circle Lazy Seven tomorrow. Call Jason if you want, and have him fly to Denver a day early. We can pick him up and head home."

She nodded in relief and squeezed Tucker's hand. "He'd like that."

He ran his thumb across her knuckles. "But, Cassie, I can't tell you I won't ride another bull. It's what I do."

Her chin lifted. "What about the concussions? Leech said a doctor told you not to ride any more after what happened in Florida."

"Leech should learn to keep his mouth shut."

"Tucker!"

"Hell, Cassie, they don't know anything for sure. You could have fifty concussions and it not affect you, or one and get punch-drunk two weeks later. You never know."

"My point exactly. You don't know how many it'll take, so quit while you're ahead."

He lifted her hand to his lips. "I'll promise you this—I won't ride another bull as long as you're around."

Her eyes got huge. "You know I can't stay with you. You've known that all along."

"All I'm saying is when you leave, you give up any claim on my life."

She looked so scared he figured she'd turn tail and run. But she didn't. She cleared her throat and said, "I didn't know I had any claim on your life now."

"Well, like it or not, you do."

"I...I..."

He smiled and tugged her down against his left side. "You don't have to say anything. I didn't say I'm in love with you. But, hell, I can't get you out of my mind."

She sighed and relaxed against the left side of his chest. "I have to admit that you're pretty high up on my list of things to think about, too. But it's because we've never made love." She threw him a nasty look. "And our prospects don't look good for the near future."

His one good arm rubbed her back. "With a little luck and
a sharp ear, we could probably manage to—"

"In a hospital? Are you crazy? No, don't bother answering.
I know you're crazy. You ride bulls." As she laid her head
back over his arm to look up at him, her braid slid over his
skin like a silk rope. "You blew it tonight, bucko. You might
as well go to sleep."

"You're staying with me, right?"

"I shouldn't. I should go back to the hotel room we're
paying for and take a long, hot bath to soothe my nerves."
She heaved a dramatic sigh. "But I guess I should stay to
keep you from doing chin-ups on the door frame."

He rested his chin on the top of her head. "This is as far
as my chin's going, right here."

Chapter Nine

"The gate is to the left just around this curve," Tucker said.

Jason leaned forward from the rear seat of Tucker's extended-cab truck. Tucker had left it at the Denver Airport when he'd flown to New York, so they hadn't needed anyone from the ranch to pick them up. But because of Tucker's injury, Cassie had insisted on driving.

She slowed as she rounded the night-darkened curve, then pulled through the arched gateway. The headlights caught the wrought-iron sign that proclaimed this the Circle Lazy Seven Ranch. A large barn stood to the left just past the entrance, but it was shut tight.

"It's another mile to the house," Tucker told them.

Cassie drove slowly along the winding gravel road as Jason plied Tucker with questions. How many cattle did he run? What breed? How many cows would an acre support? Did Tucker use artificial insemination breeding for his cows or did he prefer the natural method?

Tucker answered his questions easily, but Cassie was amazed at the details her brother knew.

"How do you know so much about ranch operations?" she asked him.

"Sam and me did some research on the Internet," Jason replied.

"I should've known," Cassie murmured.

When she drove over a hill a moment later, Jason's arm shot between the front bucket seats, finger pointed. "There it is."

Halfway down the hill a small house, dark except for the porch light, hunkered against the landscape, taking shelter from the cold night air.

Cassie eased her foot from the gas, but Tucker said, "That's the old ranch house. Roy and Eileen live there now. My house is just around—there."

Ablaze with lights, Tucker's two-story log house sat at the head of a narrow valley. Cassie couldn't tell a lot about it in the dark, but it was easily three times the size of the house they'd just passed.

"What's that line of trees?" she asked.

"Kiowa Creek. Rivers and creeks are about the only place trees grow in this neck of the woods. You'll be able to see better come morning."

"I'm looking forward to it," she told him.

"Yeah, me, too," Jason said. "We're really going to ride tomorrow, right?"

Tucker chuckled. "I'm going to insist."

"Cool."

As Cassie pulled the truck around the back of the house per Tucker's instructions, people spilled from the back door.

"Looks like they've been expecting you," Cassie said.

"Who are they?" Jason asked.

"Looks like everybody. Roy, Eileen, and all the hands." He returned Eileen's wave as Cassie turned off the engine.

Before she could put her hand on the latch, the truck door swung open. A short, lean man with a weathered face smiled at her. "Welcome to the Circle Lazy Seven, ma'am. I'm Roy Gluck. This here's my wife, Eileen."

"I'm pleased to meet you both," Cassie said as she allowed Roy's firm grip to help her down from the cab. She turned and pointed at Jason, who climbed out on Tucker's side. "I'm Cassie Burch, and that's my brother, Jason Warner."

Cassie listened quietly as Tucker satisfied their curiosity about his sling, but Eileen shook her head and snorted in disgust. "Another dadburn injury. When you gonna learn that bulls are bigger, tougher and meaner than you, boy?"

It was evidently an old argument because Tucker merely shrugged, then introduced Cassie and Jason to the men behind the Glucks. There were three permanent hands and two teenage boys the Glucks had taken in.

As the men started talking about Tucker's bull ride, Eileen touched Cassie's arm. "Come on in the house. Men ain't got enough sense to come in outta the cold."

Cassie followed the tiny woman into a large, modern kitchen that smelled like kitchens should—of yeast bread and delicious things simmering on the stove.

"You hungry?" Eileen asked.

"No, we ate in Denver."

The older woman nodded, but reached into the cabinet for bowls. She must've seen Cassie's puzzled look, because she chuckled and said, "If I know Tucker—and I do—he'll be hankering for some of my stew. I bet that brother of yours can eat something, too."

Cassie smiled wryly. "Lately it seems like Jason can always eat."

The back door opened and Tucker exclaimed, "Do I smell stew?"

Eileen glanced at Cassie, and both grinned. In that instant, Cassie knew she'd found a friend. Eileen knew more things about Tucker than Cassie could possibly learn during her short stay, but she wanted to know everything—his favorite color, what he was like before he had his morning coffee, how he liked his eggs cooked, how he treated his dogs…

Cassie's smile faded.

This sudden thirst for knowledge meant she cared about Tucker a whole lot more than she wanted to, when she'd been trying her best not to care at all.

"I'm dishing up a bowl now," Eileen called.

Tucker entered the kitchen with Jason and Roy. All three had taken off their hats. Two of the ranch hands passed behind them with the bags.

As Tucker entered the room, his eyes automatically sought Cassie's.

She felt the familiar pangs of desire and shook away her apprehension. It was just her libido again. Relieved to have an acceptable explanation, she asked, "Where are the rest of the hands? Aren't they eating?"

"They went on up to the bunkhouse," Roy told her. "We didn't know when you'd be gettin' in, so we ate an hour ago."

"Cassie, could you pour coffee?" Eileen asked as she set two large bowls of stew on the kitchen table. "I made an apple pie this afternoon. Why don't you cut a piece for yourself?"

Cassie looked around for a coffeemaker and was amazed to find the pot on the stove. She didn't know anyone made coffee like that anymore. She poured four cups for the adults and milk for Jason, then cut a small sliver of pie just to be polite.

The pie melted in Cassie's mouth as Tucker and Roy discussed the business of the ranch and the new bunkhouse. Her heart swelled with pride at Tucker's selflessness. He was using the money he earned to help boys who were growing up the way he had.

As she listened to Tucker and Roy discuss the plans, affection and mutual respect were evident in every word the two men spoke.

Jason paid careful attention while he ate every bite of stew. His interest in Tucker and the ranch both delighted and worried Cassie. On the one hand, she hadn't seen her brother this animated in a long time. On the other, she knew it couldn't last. Even if Jason's interest didn't wane, they eventually had to return to New York where ranches were in short supply.

Jason and Tucker finished the large pieces of pie Eileen cut for them, then Roy announced it was time for the couple to leave.

"Just leave those dishes in the sink," Eileen said as she slipped into her jacket. "I'll take care of 'em in the mornin'."

When the door closed behind them, Jason asked in amazement, "Did he really stick his arm inside that horse to pull out the baby?"

Tucker nodded. "Happens all the time, Tick. 'Specially with first-time mamas, which this mare was. Had a hard time gettin' her with foal, and a hard time gettin' the foal out."

"Cool. I mean, it's not cool that she had a hard time but... You know."

Tucker chuckled and leaned back in his chair. "We've got another mare ready to foal any day now. You want to watch?"

Jason's eyes shone. "You bet."

"Could be two o'clock in the morning."

"I don't care."

"I'll tell Roy." Tucker stacked his coffee mug on his plate, then rose and tried to pick up both with his one good hand.

Jason saved the mug as it fell, then took all of Tucker's dishes to the sink, as well as his own. Was this the same brother who left empty chip bags and half-drunk soda cans in her living room?

"Want a tour of the house?" Tucker asked her.

"Sure."

He showed them around the downstairs rooms, obviously proud of his home. Cassie liked the rustic charm of the log walls and Western decor. The rooms felt warm and inviting, and fit Tucker's personality as well as his black hat. They lost Jason to Tucker's computer when they left the ranch office.

Tucker's good hand took Cassie's as they climbed the stairs. "I'll show you to your room."

"So, you didn't put me in with you," she said on a sigh.

"You don't have to sound so relieved."

"It's not that." She laced her fingers through his and leaned closer. "But with Jason here, we have to be as careful as we were in New York."

"I know," he rumbled. "On top of that, Eileen's old-fashioned. If Jason weren't here to chaperone, I have no doubt that she'd be flouting Roy's wishes and sleeping in the room between ours. Let's see…" He opened the first door. "Yep, here's your suitcase. My room's there at the end of the hall. Let's see if she put Jason in between… Yep."

"They're nice rooms," she said. "Jason and I share a bath?"

He grinned and put his good arm around her shoulders. "Unless you want to come use the Whirlpool in the master bath."

She leaned against him wearily. The last two days felt like two weeks. Neither of them got much sleep the night before at the hospital. "Sounds good. I might take you up on that offer."

He bent to kiss her. "Just let me know and I'll wash your back."

Cassie moaned softly at the feel of his lips on hers. Right now, she just wanted to sink into his warmth and stay there indefinitely. "One-handed?"

"Angel, I'll use as many hands as I've got at the time."

The next day, the sound of Tucker's deep voice drew Cassie around the edge of the barn. She stopped abruptly at the corner, her eyes widening as they fell on her brother. With a rope in his hands, Jason ran around the corral, his attention on the horses that shied away from him.

Tucker leaned against the railing. "That palomino's the one you want."

"Why don't they stand still?" Jason asked, breathing hard.

"Hell, they don't want to work any more than you do, Tick."

Cassie eased up beside Tucker. He smiled and slipped his left arm around her shoulders.

She frowned up at him. "We have to catch our own horses?"

"You don't." He nodded to his right where a mottled gray horse tied to the corral stood patiently. "Sally Bee's saddled and ready to go."

"So why is Jason chasing one down?"

"'Cause I told him to." Tucker raised his voice. "You'll never catch him by running at his head. Ease up on him."

"Is this some ritual you put new riders through?" she asked.

Tucker shrugged and called to Jason, "Let him know you're not going to hurt him. This horse doesn't know you. Not yet. But by the end of this week, you're gonna be bosom buddies."

"Why aren't you making me chase mine? It's because I'm a woman, isn't it?" Cassie's eyes narrowed. "Let me tell you one thing, Tucker Reeves. I can chase a horse as well as—"

He leaned over and stopped her with a kiss. "It's not because you're a woman. It's because you're not a thirteen-year-old boy. He's learning things out there he won't learn anyplace else. And look at him... Do you hear him complaining?"

Cassie watched as Jason got within several feet of the palomino. He reached out with the loop and had it half over the horse's nose before another horse whinnied and the palomino backed out of range. Jason slammed the dirt with one boot and pushed the black hat Tucker had given him a little higher. Then he went after the horse again.

"He may not be complaining," Cassie said. "But he doesn't look like he's having fun, either."

"Hell, he's having more fun than ten Mortal Kombat games, 'cause this is real life. He's learning that living, breathing creatures can't be controlled with the flick of a joystick."

Jason whooped loudly then, proving Tucker's statement. Cassie felt as if an invisible hand squeezed her heart. But the emotion urging her to slip her arms around Tucker was just gratitude. It had to be. She felt this way because Tucker was helping her brother. It was natural for her to like anyone who helped, right?

No, it wasn't natural. Not for Cassie. She believed in depending on no one but herself.

So why did Tucker's help mean so much?

Maybe she wasn't as independent as she thought. Was it possible her insistence on independence was just habit? That she insisted on doing everything for herself because she'd never had anyone to help her?

Uncomfortable with the possibility that the entire structure of her life was based on something so nebulous, she told herself that Tucker's help had absolutely nothing to do with her or how she felt—it was about Jason. Jason needed help, wherever it came from. It didn't matter whether or not Cassie hated asking for help. Her brother's happiness was worth any price.

She frowned. That was the problem. The "price" wasn't a burden at all. Being around Tucker, accepting his help, trusting his judgment, seemed so natural, so right. She liked trusting him.

That, more than anything, made her suspect her independence might be a sham. That, more than anything, scared her spitless.

To distract herself, she lifted her camera and took several shots of Jason. "How long's this going to take?"

"Shouldn't be too long. See? The gelding's letting him closer every—"

"Got him!"

Jason grinned and held up the rope, the loop secure around the palomino's neck. The horse calmly followed as the boy led him across the corral. Jason walked with a swagger that Cassie recognized. It was an exact mimic of Tucker's gait.

She didn't know whether to laugh, cry, or run screaming back to New York.

As the men and boys settled around the long dining room table for lunch, Tucker marched back into the kitchen and demanded, "Where's Cassie?"

Eileen shook her wooden spoon at him. "You done wore her out, Tucker Reeves. She ain't one of these tough young men we bring out to the ranch. You can't throw a woman like Cassie on the back of a horse and expect her to gallop off into the sunset."

Tucker frowned. "I put her on Sally Bee. She's the oldest, gentlest mare we've got."

"I know. She's the one I ride when I got to. But when you're not used to being in a saddle, even her gait is mighty jarrin'."

"Is she hurt real bad? She said she was fine."

"And what's she gonna say when you cowboys wouldn't say nothing if you had an arrow sticking out of your head?" Eileen shook her head and tsked. "She ain't too bad off yet. I sent her upstairs to soak in that fancy tub of yours. I was gonna send Stretch over to our place to fetch that liniment of mine after lunch."

"I'll go right now." Tucker stepped into the mudroom for his hat. "Where is it?"

"On the top shelf of the medicine cabinet, in a blue jar. Can't miss it."

Tucker nodded and strode out the door. He took his arm out of the sling and swung up on the bay gelding Stretch had left tied to the hitching post. His shoulder complained at the strain of lifting himself into the saddle, but he soon forgot about it.

He was back at his own house in twenty minutes. Lunch was in full swing but everyone was too busy eating to notice him, so he quietly slipped upstairs. The hum of the Whirlpool greeted him as he eased open the door to his bedroom.

"Cassie?" he called softly.

His concern deepened when he got no reply. He placed the jar of liniment on the dresser and pushed open the door to the bathroom. Warm moist air swirled around him, perfumed with the scent of roses.

His chest caught a lungful at the sight of Cassie reclining like a goddess in the faux marble tub. Her titian tresses were gathered on top of her head. A few strands fell in artful disarray over the lip of the tub.

The vision drew Tucker forward like clover draws honeybees. His heartbeat increased speed with every step, and his temperature rose disproportionately to the heat in the room. As he approached, a rivulet of water traveled a circuitous path around the beads on her flushed skin—all the way from her shoulder to the deep cleft between her breasts. His eyes tracked the droplet's course until it melded with the bubbling water.

Hot blood surged through him, and desire stabbed into his gut. He felt green and raw, as if he'd never had a woman before. But at the same time he felt as if he'd known *this* woman in every way possible.

He stood over her for long minutes, mesmerized by the dancing water that played over her curves, revealing the roundness of a breast here, the shadow at the apex of her legs there—only to snatch the brief glimpses away.

He didn't know what he did to alert her, but her eyes suddenly opened. As she stared mutely up at him, the green color changed hues—from the bright green of surprise, to the murky depths of desire.

Cassie's eyes ran up the misty, blue jeans-clad figure.

Was Tucker really here, gazing at her like a starving man at a feast? Or had the heat gone to her head?

Tucker dropped to his heels and reached for a red curl plastered to her shoulder. "You hurtin' bad?"

The light brush of his fingers against her skin made the heat surrounding her sink all the way to her bones. He was very,

very real. Her voice was husky as she lifted a wet hand to his cheek. "Not at the moment."

Tucker leaned forward slowly, watching her lips as she parted them and lifted them to meet his.

The first touch was like a butterfly landing softly on the petals of a rose. Cassie sighed against him. She couldn't tell if the warm, wet heat fogging her brain came from him or the tub, but it didn't matter.

Desire pounded through her. When he ran his tongue along her teeth, she opened her mouth and wrapped her arms around his neck. His tongue thrust against hers, twirling, demanding she join the dance.

She had no intention of denying him.

Falling to his knees for better balance, Tucker reached into the water and slipped his arms around her back, heedless of his shirt. As her tongue twined with his, he half lifted her from the water. She took the hint and gathered her legs beneath her.

"Your shoulder doesn't hurt?" she asked breathlessly.

"Not at the moment."

They rose together. Tucker felt rational thought melt away as Cassie's wet body molded to his. The smooth, slick, flushed skin sliding beneath his hands reminded him of her other body parts he wanted to touch. Running his hands down her back and over the firm mounds of her bottom, he squeezed.

"Owww!"

Chapter Ten

Tucker released Cassie immediately and pulled back, only to grab her around the waist as she nearly slipped. "Damn. Why did you tell me you weren't hurting?"

"I didn't hurt until you grabbed me."

Tucker groaned and leaned his forehead against hers. "I'm sorry. I forget how sore greenhorns get their first day out." He released a ragged breath. "It's just as well you stopped me. There's a houseful of people at the dining table downstairs."

Cassie took several deep breaths, then arched her neck to look at him. "Greenhorn, huh?"

He smiled. "Like it or not, that's what you are."

She sniffed. "So is Jason, and he rode longer than I did. Isn't he sore?"

"If he is, he's not going to admit it. But I'm sure he'll be walking funny tomorrow. Good thing Eileen's got enough liniment for both of you. Come on. I'll help you rub some in."

She arched a brow. "It's my butt that's sore."

His face tightened. "I know."

"But we haven't ever… I mean, you haven't touched me… Are you sure?"

"No, but it's the least I can do. It'll be my penance for not taking better care of you." He grabbed a towel and wrapped it around her. "I'll let you return the favor. After I rub you, you can massage some into my shoulder. Okay?"

"Okay."

When he leaned down to lift her in his arms, she stepped back. "Oh, no, you don't. Not with your shoulder. I can walk."

She did hold on to his arm when she stepped from the tub, though. As she turned toward the bedroom, he bent to turn off the Whirlpool action and drain the tub.

"Is the liniment in this blue jar?" she called.

"Yes, ma'am."

When he entered the bedroom, she had the lid off and the jar under her nose. "Not exactly Chanel Number Five, but it's not as bad as I expected."

Tucker took the jar and pointed at the bed. "Facedown."

Cassie glanced at the bed, then at him. "You sure?"

He nodded, and she climbed onto the king-size mattress.

At the sight of her stretching out on his bed—where he'd imagined her countless times—he groaned.

She looked as if she belonged.

But she didn't. The fact that he was about to rub liniment on her sore bottom told him she was too delicate for ranch life. Too soft for a lout like him.

Who needs you?

How many times did those words have to echo in his brain before he believed them?

Had he made a mistake bringing Cassie to his ranch? After she left, he'd never be able to look at his bed, or his bathtub, or his kitchen, or even that old mare Sally Bee without thinking of Cassie. Without wanting her.

She twisted to look up at him. "Second thoughts?"

"Yep. But I can handle it."

He shook his head to rid himself of regret. He'd deal with whatever pain losing her brought when it came around. He had her now. That's all that mattered.

That evening, Tucker pushed open the back door and glanced down the porch. Cassie stood at one end, a dark shape against a starlit sky. He closed the door and walked over to her.

She sighed as he pulled her back against his chest. "It's beautiful here."

He pushed her braid over her shoulder and kissed the nape of her neck. "I'm glad you like it."

"So many stars. You don't see very many in New York."

"You've got more people, we've got more stars."

"Mmm."

"So..." he whispered close to her ear. "Which do you prefer?"

Her head twisted down and away. He could feel her wince more than see it, and felt like kicking himself. "I'm sorry. I shouldn't—"

The back door creaked open. Tucker's head turned to see J.C. and Glen step onto the porch. With a skilled hunter's instincts, Glen saw him immediately. He nodded at Tucker as J.C. lit a cigarette. Tucker pulled Cassie closer and shifted to shield her from their view.

The ranch hands meandered toward their bunkhouse.

"How's your shoulder?" she asked before he could renew the conversation.

"Fine. How's your rump?"

"Fine."

He let a hand travel down her hip to gently squeeze the roundness he'd massaged so diligently a few hours earlier.

She sucked in a quick breath, but not in pleasure.

"Liar," he breathed.

"Well, it's better than it was." She chuckled and twisted again to look up at him. "We're a sorry pair, aren't we?"

His lips found hers unerringly in the darkness. His shoulder twinged as he brought a hand up to support her head, but the pain was insignificant compared to the fire that burned paths down every blood vessel in his body. His tongue met hers, twining, dancing, searing all thought from his brain.

"Ahem."

Tucker's head snapped around to see Stretch standing in the open door. "What is it?"

"Sorry, boss. Roy and I were just talking about them strays over to Crocker's Bend. He wants to know if you want us to fetch 'em tomorrow, 'fore they become too wild."

"Hell, I don't know. What would he do if I weren't here?"

"He'd fetch 'em."

"Then go get them."

Stretch nodded and went back into the house.

Tucker leaned his forehead on Cassie's. "There's too damn many people around this place."

She ran a hand over his cheek. "But they're nice people."

"I know. Roy tries to include me in decisions when I'm home. Tries to make me feel like I'm part of the place."

"Of course you're part of it. You own it, don't you?"

"Straight-out. But sometimes..." Tucker shifted his eyes to the barn sitting down the hill, half a football field away from the house. He wasn't sure he wanted to continue. He'd never shared these thoughts with anyone.

"Sometimes what?" she urged softly.

He sighed. He shouldn't have started what he didn't want to finish. Not with Cassie. "Sometimes I feel like I don't belong here. That it's Roy's ranch, not mine."

"Why?"

"It's my fault. I haven't been around much. Too busy chasing gold buckles."

"Roy must know you feel this way, if he tries to include you."

Tucker ran his hands back from her face, smoothing down strands of hair that had escaped her braid. "Roy seems to

know everything. That's one reason I hired him. Sometimes I
think he can read people's minds. Hell, I know he can read
the minds of cows and horses.''

Cassie turned to fully face him. She wrapped her hands
around his waist and leaned into his chest. ''So where do you
belong?''

With you.

The words popped into his mind before he could stop them.
But he knew he couldn't say them—might never be able to
say them. Misery flooded through him, and he laid his chin
on the top of her head. The wisps of hair that wouldn't stay
down tickled his neck. ''Hell, I don't know. On the back of a
bull's the only place I've ever felt at home.''

''And now you can't ride bulls anymore.''

''Not supposed to, no.''

She pulled him so close, he couldn't tell where his heat
ended and hers began. ''You need to stay home more than a
few days at a time. The people here love you. They want you
around more.''

Tucker smiled. ''You've been talking to Eileen.''

He could feel her smile against his chest. ''I like her.''

They stood silently for several minutes, enjoying the night,
enjoying each other. Tucker knew neither one of them was up
to any sexual acrobatics that night, which was just as well
with a ranch full of people. But he liked being with Cassie.
He liked talking to her, teasing her, kissing her.

''Let's go for a walk,'' he suggested.

She pulled back just enough to peer up at him. ''Tucker,
we can't—''

''I know. But we can do everything else.''

She searched his face, though he didn't know what she
could see in the darkness. Finally she said softly, ''All right.''

He grinned. ''I'll get our coats.''

''How you holdin' up?'' Tucker asked the next day as they
rode toward Colter Ridge.

Cassie pulled her gaze from the view of the distant snow-capped Rocky Mountains. They were going to make a great backdrop for the photos. A cowboy in his element.

She smiled at the cowboy in question. "I think I'm actually getting the hang of riding. Who knows? I may not even need the liniment tonight."

Tucker's grin was so knowing and sexy, she felt heat crawling up her neck and face. "Don't say that. Rubbing it in is my favorite part of the day."

It was Cassie's, too, but she wasn't going to admit that.

"A penny for your thoughts."

"Oh, I think you could save your money on this one," she told him with a wry smile. "You know exactly what I'm thinking."

He urged his horse closer to hers and reached for her hand. "We'll get a chance soon."

She felt the warmth of his hand even through the gloves she wore against the chill. "When? This is our fourth day here and we haven't been able to do more than kiss. The midnight trip to the hayloft didn't work because Stretch, Roy and Jason were camped in there waiting on that mare to foal. When you made a pallet under the stars not only was it too cold to take off our clothes, we were nearly stepped on by a cow."

His hand squeezed hers, then he let go as the horses had to maneuver around a large rock. "Jason's been getting on with Jimmy and Mike the last couple of days. Maybe he'd like to spend the night in the bunkhouse."

She brightened. "I bet he'd jump at the chance."

Tucker nodded. "We probably won't even have to be subtle. Let's suggest it at supper. Maybe he'll like it so much he'll stay there the rest of the week."

Cassie squirmed in the saddle. She'd believe it when she had Tucker naked in her arms.

"So, how much further?" she asked.

"We're almost there."

"I can't shoot anything without my equipment. I don't

know why you had to put it in Jason's saddlebags. Where are the boys, anyway?''

"They'll meet us there. They're not going to poke along with us when they can go the long way around."

"Jason will be okay with them, won't he? He's only been riding three days. He's not—"

"He'll be fine. Jimmy's been around long enough to know the ropes. He'll take care of Jason. If he doesn't, Roy'll have him mucking stalls for a month, and he knows it."

"You mean, he doesn't muck stalls now? You said everyone had to clean up after their own horse."

"Everyone doesn't have to when one of the boys screws up 'cause Roy makes 'em muck everybody's stall. The hands love it when that happens. They think they're on vacation."

"I wouldn't be surprised if your ranch hands encourage the boys to get in trouble," she said. "Especially J.C. He seems like he loves a prank."

"You pegged him right. But J.C. knows if Roy found out, he'd be mucking right along with the boys." Tucker pulled his horse to a stop. "Here we are. What do you think?"

Cassie carefully pulled on Sally Bee's reins until she stopped. Colter Ridge was higher than the surrounding hills. The view of the distant Rockies took her breath away. "It's perfect. You think the boys will be long? I don't want to lose this light."

"They better not be, or I'll have 'em all mucking stalls."

Tucker swung out of the saddle, then grabbed Cassie around the waist and lifted her down. He didn't let go, but pulled her against him and covered her mouth with his.

She leaned into him with a sigh. When she tried to wrap her hands around his neck, the reins in one hand pulled her up short.

"What about the horses?" she asked between kisses.

Tucker trailed kisses across to her ear. "What horses?"

His warm mouth gently sucking on the lobe of her ear

burned away all thought of horses until Sally Bee dropped her head to graze and yanked Cassie half out of Tucker's arms.

Cassie shook her head to clear the haze of desire, then chuckled. "These horses."

"Damned old nag," Tucker muttered. He took Sally Bee's reins and pulled her head up. "Let me hobble them, then we can get back to—"

"Tucker!" Mike rode up the hill at a full gallop. He yanked the black mare to a stop just yards away, making their horses shy and pull at their reins. "Jason's horse slid down a ravine."

Chapter Eleven

"Oh, my God. Jason!" Cassie's heart stopped beating. "Is he…"

Mike's face pinched. "He wasn't moving."

"No!" Cassie screamed.

Tucker thrust Sally Bee's reins into Cassie's hands, then swung into his saddle. "Where is he?"

"On the other side of Double-Naught Hill, that ravine with the deep wash." The boy swung his mare's head around. "I've got to get back to Jimmy."

"No," Tucker yelled. When the boy stopped, Tucker told him, "You're going to stay behind and ride with Cassie."

"But I told Jimmy…" Mike trailed off at Tucker's hard look. "Aw, hell."

Tucker glanced down at Cassie. "I'm riding as hard as I can. Mike will take you."

He spurred the bay gelding and was gone.

Cassie watched until Tucker disappeared over a hill, praying as hard as she could.

"Ma'am?"

She looked back to see Mike standing beside her.

"I was gonna help you mount, if that's okay."

"What happened?" she demanded.

A guilty look made Mike wince. "I'm awful sorry—for real and true. Jimmy and me jumped the ravine. We was showing off in front of Tick, I guess. But, dang it, we didn't know he'd try, too."

Cassie's hand tightened on the reins. "Jason will try anything."

The boy nodded miserably. "I should'a knowed. He ain't much different from me when I come here."

She put a hand on his shoulder. "Let's go."

Mike helped her mount, then swung into his saddle. He started out at a trot but Cassie couldn't wait. She spurred Sally Bee past his mare, ignoring the panicked feeling of bouncing over the hard earth as it swept past below. Mike took the hint, and the lead.

Sally Bee was breathing hard when Mike slowed at the top of a hill.

"There," he called, pointing below and to the left.

Two male figures and two horses stood above the narrow end of a gorge that stretched away to the east. Cassie recognized the gelding Tucker had been riding, but the two figures were too much alike for either one of them to be him.

"Isn't that Jason?" she asked.

"Yes, ma'am," Mike yelled with a grin. "He's okay."

Relief swept through her. "Where's Tucker?"

"He must be in the ravine, seeing about the horse."

Cassie kicked the mare, urging her down the hill. Jason and Jimmy glanced up once, then turned their attention back to the gully. When she pulled Sally Bee to a stop, Cassie slid from the saddle and ran to her brother.

She didn't even stop to think about it as she hugged him close and whispered, "Thank God, you're okay."

Jason fidgeted in her arms. "Aw, Cassie."

She released her death grip, but grabbed his shoulders and looked him over. A trail of blood ran from under his hat, which she swept off. A knot was already forming in the hair at his temple. "You're hurt."

A feeling of sick helplessness cascaded over her. Nothing could have proven to her more that she and Jason didn't belong on a ranch. There were so many dangers. True, there were dangers in New York, but she knew what they were and could help him avoid them. Out here...

What if she'd been alone? How could she have helped Jason? She couldn't even ride fast enough to keep up with Tucker.

Jason fended off the hand she lifted to his face. "I'm okay. You should be worried about my horse. Jimmy said I might've crippled him. They might have to..." His developing Adam's apple bobbed. "Tucker's checking him out."

Another wave of emotion threatened to choke Cassie. Her brother was growing up. Instead of hiding his feelings like a kid trying to be cool, he let his compassion for the injured horse show. She couldn't resist giving him one more hug, then she released him.

As she turned toward the ravine, she caught Mike watching them. He quickly glanced away, but not before she saw his hungry fascination. Cassie's heart went out to the boy who'd grown up with little or no affection. He needed hugs and kisses as much as anybody, probably more.

His need overcame her natural reluctance. She walked over to Mike and pulled him into her arms.

He stiffened. "What's that for?"

"For coming to get us quickly, even though you knew you're going to get in trouble. And for staying behind with me."

"Okay, okay, okay, okay."

But he let her hold on until scrambling sounds from the ravine drew their attention. Seconds later, Tucker emerged at the top.

He rolled his sore shoulder as if to shake off the pain climbing caused, then he passed a hard look around at all three boys, ending with Jason. "The palomino's not hurt bad. He lost a couple of shoes, and looks like he sprained a hip muscle. But it's a miracle, and we're gonna have a helluva time getting him out without further injury."

Jason lifted his chin manfully. "What do we need to do?"

Tucker nodded toward the north. "Roy and J.C. are working up along Hungry Horse Creek. Jimmy, go fetch them. Mike, you ride in and tell Stretch to bring the truck around to the ravine. The closest place he can get to is about half a mile east. He'll know the place. Tell him to bring every rope and winch he can lay his hands on. Jason, that's your horse. You get down there and—"

"What?" Cassie stepped forward. "Jason's not going to do anything but ride back to the house with—"

"No, I'm not," Jason argued.

"The hell he is," Tucker said at the same time.

Her eyes narrowed. "He's hurt. He needs—"

"He sure doesn't need coddling," Tucker said mercilessly. "He needs to learn that his actions have consequences. How's he gonna learn that if you take him back to a nice, soft bed?"

"He was knocked out," she argued. "He needs to see a doctor."

Jason stepped in front of her. "I wasn't knocked out."

Her eyes narrowed. "Mike said you weren't moving."

Jason gave Mike a dirty look.

Mike's face reddened, and he swung up on his horse. "Come on, Jimmy, we'd better get going."

Jason turned back to Cassie. "I had my breath knocked out, is all."

"There's a knot on your head the size of my fist."

"Okay, I hit my head on a rock, but it didn't knock me out." Jason planted his hands on his hips. "I'm staying here, Cassie. My horse needs me. Tucker needs me." He glanced at Tucker. "Right?"

Tucker nodded, his face softening. "Yes, sir, I do."

Cassie held a couple of fingers in front of Jason's eyes. "How many?"

"Two," he answered without hesitation.

"All right, we'll stay. Maybe I can at least get some decent shots while you're working to get that poor horse—" Suddenly she groaned. "My cameras are still in your saddlebags, aren't they?"

A sick look came over Jason's face. "I hope so."

Tucker flicked off the rodeo videotape he'd been watching as Cassie came down the stairs. "How's Jason?"

"The aspirin didn't help his head much," she replied. "I came down to get some ice to make a cold pack. It's probably too late to ease the swelling of that bump, but it might relieve the pain a little."

"I'll help you." Tucker started to get up but Cassie hurried over and held him down. It didn't take much pressure.

"No, you won't. You worked harder than anybody today. I know you're bone-tired. And your shoulder's got to be hurting, too."

Tucker sank back against the cushions. Every muscle in his body hurt from hauling the palomino out of the ravine, and his shoulder screamed every time he moved it. "A little."

"I'll rub you down with liniment after I give Jason the ice pack."

He grinned up at her. "All over?"

She leaned down and kissed him. "As much as you can stand."

She went into the kitchen, then back upstairs. He was relieved she wasn't mad at him for making Jason stick around and help.

She returned in fifteen minutes. He peeled off his shirt and sat on the edge of the couch, between her legs. The heat of the liniment slowly sank into his shoulder under the firm ministrations of her fingers.

He wished she'd never stop.

Finally she screwed the lid on the jar. "If you'll lay on your stomach, I'll massage your back, except for right here." She leaned forward and placed a gentle kiss on his back where the frightened gelding had kicked him.

He shivered at the sweetness of the caress and asked hopefully, "Don't you need me to rub liniment on you?"

"No, I'm fine. Tonight you're the one who needs help." She slowly ran her fingers up through his hair. "We can't do anything, anyway. Jason's headache is keeping him from sleeping."

Tucker ignored his muscles' complaints as he twisted and kissed her.

She smiled at him tenderly, then rubbed a hand back through his hair. "Lie down, cowboy."

The soft, sultry way she said "cowboy" made Tucker's heart swell with emotion. As endearments went, it wasn't overwhelming. But she said it the same way wives called their husbands "honey" or "sweetheart."

Who needs you?

The question that had haunted him since his parents died got weaker the longer Cassie stayed. He was beginning to hope his very own angel had alighted atop his Christmas tree—and would stay long past December.

Did that mean he was falling in love?

Probably, though it wasn't one of his smarter moves. Cassie was leaving the Circle Lazy Seven in five days. She was going to walk right out of his life.

He didn't know if it would be easier to tell her he was falling in love with her, or not to tell her. So he did neither, just tried to keep things light. "You just want me to lie down so you can have your way with me."

"Don't you wish." She scraped a fingernail down the stubble on his jaw. "Don't I wish."

Tucker kissed her again, then stretched out on the couch. She straddled his hips and massaged his aching muscles. Within minutes, he was asleep.

* * *

The next day Cassie meandered onto the back porch and took a deep breath of crisp evening air. The sun had just disappeared over the Rockies, leaving the sky streaked with pinks and purples.

Funny, the things you didn't realize you were missing, living in New York. The only sunsets she'd seen in the past ten years were ones she was shooting in some far-off location. And those she only saw through the lens of her camera. They were just composition and light to her. They didn't take her breath away or make her feel like...like there was magic in the air.

Cassie blinked, startled. Where had that thought come from? But she had to admit she loved the Circle Lazy Seven. Though she sometimes felt as if she didn't belong, other times it seemed as if she'd lived here all her life. She felt really, truly alive for the first time.

The hustle and bustle of New York and the nonstop pace of her career had only given her the illusion of being alive. But she didn't know if she'd be satisfied with living on the fringes of life anymore. She wanted to watch the sunsets instead of shooting them. She wanted to taste the ice cream instead of watching it melt under hot studio lights. She wanted to be involved in the lives of the people here on the Circle Lazy Seven. She wanted... Tucker.

Though he'd never said the words, he made her feel as if she were more important to him than sunlight. She liked being the center of his universe, and she wanted the feeling to continue for more than the few weeks they'd bargained for.

Was she in love? She had no idea. She only knew that though she'd never believed in forever, now forever didn't seem so bad.

If only she had the courage to gamble for what she wanted. If only the thought of making such a huge commitment didn't scare her so much she could hardly breathe. If only she just had herself to worry about.

She was fairly certain her career would stand a move west. Her best work—the photos that won awards—were all shot on location. That was where she was at her best. The Denver airport was only an hour away. She could be on location as fast as the models. And she knew she could get as much studio work as she could handle from agencies in Denver. She had credentials, after all, and New York references.

No, it wasn't her career she was worried about. It was Jason.

Her brother needed a stable home. He'd been moved around so much during his short life—from town to town, friends to friends, father to father. He didn't need more of the same.

If she moved to Colorado with him, she'd be doing the same thing their mother did to them both.

Sure, her relationship with Tucker might work. They might live together happily for the next fifty years. But the odds were against it. She knew from personal experience. She'd lived with those odds for nineteen years.

If she were on her own, she might try to beat the odds. But she didn't have the right to risk Jason's happiness, too.

As if he knew she'd been thinking about him, Jason suddenly rounded the corner of the house—coming from the barn and smelling like one.

When he saw her, he stopped dead. His face was flushed and tight with anger. Misery shone like tears in his eyes. "I hate it here."

Cassie leaned on the porch rail. "What happened?"

For an answer, he turned around. From his neck to his butt, he was covered in manure.

The chuckle that escaped Cassie was instinctive. She clamped her hand over her mouth as Jason spun around and glared at her.

"It's not funny!"

"I know it isn't to you," she said. "But it's some wacky law of human nature that we all laugh when someone steps or falls into an offending substance. Probably known as the Three Stooges Law or something."

He threw a hand toward the barn. "Then go join the crowd. They're all laughing at me. Your boyfriend laughed the hardest."

"Tucker?" He'd been so sensitive to Jason's needs that Cassie couldn't believe he'd deliberately hurt her brother's feelings. "Surely there's a good explanation for—"

"That's it. Take his side over mine."

Cassie recognized this argument. Jason had it with their mother more times than she could count. "I'm not taking anybody's side. It's just common sense to realize that if you're going to be around cows and horses, you're going to step in a little manure. And I guess occasionally fall in it. What happened? Did you slip?"

"I was pushed," he growled. "Tucker made us muck the stalls because of what happened at the ravine yesterday. When we had a nice big pile of the stuff in the middle of the barn, they pushed me in it."

"Jimmy and Mike?"

"No. Captain Kirk and Spock."

Cassie started down the steps. "I'll go see what's going on."

"Oh, right. Cassie to the rescue." Jason stomped over and stood on the bottom step, chin high, chest out. The bump he'd received in the ravine showed as a dark bruise on his temple. "I don't need you to do my fighting for me."

"I wasn't going to fight. I was going to—"

"Just leave it alone. Okay?"

His gaze was so intense, Cassie shrugged. "All right."

The air went out of him then, and he looked like a lost little boy. Cassie tried to pull him into her arms, but he stepped back out of reach.

She sighed. Just as well, considering he was covered in manure. She nodded toward the door. "Go into the mudroom and take off your shirt and jeans. Hand them out to me and I'll hose them off while you shower."

He stomped by her into the house.

He'd just handed Cassie his clothes from the mudroom when Eileen came around the other corner of the house.

The old woman took one look at the clothes Cassie held at arm's length and grinned. "I see Jason's been initiated."

Cassie blinked. "'Initiated'?"

Eileen came slowly up the steps, chuckling. "It's a rite of passage for all the boys who come live with me and Roy. Started back with Tucker. He was sassing off to Roy one day after working hard all afternoon mucking stalls. Roy hauled off and shoved him back into the pile he'd just made. It's become a tradition since then. Sorta like being baptized."

Cassie held up the clothes. "So this is a good thing?"

"Good, clean manure never hurt nobody."

"Maybe not physically."

Eileen regarded her shrewdly. "Jason didn't cotton to the smell, I take it."

Cassie shook her head. "He thinks they did it out of meanness."

"The baptizees always do." Eileen smiled. "He go clean up? He'll be down directly, then. I'll set him in front of a piece of pie and set him straight."

"Maybe I should explain things to him. He's always been very sensitive."

Eileen shook her head. "Can't buck tradition. A piece of my pie and a piece of my mind always come after the baptizing. You planning on hosing them clothes down?"

Cassie nodded.

"I'd be much obliged." Eileen placed a hand on her arm. "Don't you worry, hon. I know what to say."

Cassie watched Eileen disappear into the mudroom. A week ago Cassie would've insisted on explaining things to Jason herself, even knowing Eileen was far better qualified.

Suddenly New York felt like a long way away—and not just in miles.

* * *

That evening, Tucker opened the door to his office and found Jason sitting at the computer. "Here you are."

The boy merely shrugged at the obvious observation. He'd been quiet since the manure incident that afternoon, but Tucker wasn't about to apologize. If Jason wanted to be a cowboy, he had to get used to the stuff.

"Didn't Jimmy and Mike come in and ask you to ride over to the Double Diamond with them?"

Jason didn't look away from the computer screen. "I hope every bronc they get on slams them down in the dirt."

"They probably will, but not because you want them to."

"You made them ask."

"The hell I did. You'd know that if you hadn't bolted from the supper table as soon as you inhaled your grub. They asked if they could take you."

The sideways glance he threw at Tucker was an odd mixture of disbelief and hope. "Probably so they could show off."

Tucker shook his head. Jason's lack of self-esteem was showing again. He thought he'd begun to build the boy's confidence, but it looked as though the baptism this afternoon had brought them back to ground zero. He regretted mentioning it to Jimmy and Mike, but he didn't know they'd take such relish in initiating Jason. "You playing games?"

Jason shook his head. "I'm sending Sam an e-mail. You said I could."

"Sure. That's fine." Tucker walked over and leaned a hip on the end of the desk. After a minute of watching Jason type, he said softly, "They're jealous of you, you know."

"Jimmy and Mike?" He snorted. "Of what? The way I ride? How good I can rope? I can't even brush down my horse without someone yelling at me for doing it wrong."

"They're not jealous of what you can do. They're jealous of what you have."

"Yeah, I'm real rich."

"I'm not talking about money, Tick. I'm talking about family. You have a sister who loves you very much. It's a helluva

lot more than either one of them has. On top of that, you sleep
here in the big house and are treated like a guest, rather than
a ranch hand.''

The boy's eyes narrowed. "How do you know what they
feel?"

"Because I felt the same way when I was their age. I hated
kids at school who had a real home, a real family. I know
you've felt it, too, growing up with no dad."

"I had five dads."

Tucker shook his head. "Having five dads is the same as
having none."

Jason didn't reply, but looked at the computer screen
thoughtfully.

"Jimmy and Mike also suggested we camp out tomorrow
night, if you're up for it. This warm spell looks like it's going
to hold."

The boy glanced up then, clearly interested. "With tents
and everything?"

"Hell, no. We sleep under the stars."

"Cool."

Tucker smiled. "You're right about that. Even though it's
warmed up some, it's still cool at night. So all three of you
will be required to take your jackets—and wear them."

"Aw, man."

"You ready for our walk?" Cassie asked from the open
door.

Tucker's eyes sought her coat-clad figure in the doorway.
They exchanged an intimate smile. He looked forward to the
strolls they took every evening after supper. After only four
days, they'd become a habit. It was the only time Tucker had
Cassie all to himself. The only time they could talk, and kiss—
and get so frustrated he couldn't sleep at night. But he
wouldn't stop going with her for all the gold buckles in the
world.

He stood. "Let me grab my coat."

"Where you guys going?" Jason asked.

"For a walk," Cassie said.

"Yeah, but where?"

"Probably along the creek," Tucker told him.

Jason nodded.

When he didn't say anything else, Cassie asked, "Do you want to go?"

"Nah. Oh, Tucker, is Cassie going on our camping trip?"

Her green eyes turned to his. "Camping trip?"

Tucker glanced at her. "It's usually men only, but if you want to go..."

"And freeze my tush off? I don't know..."

Since Jason's attention was on the computer, Tucker slipped his hand down her back to caress the gently rounded tush she referred to, and leaned close to whisper, "Don't worry. I'll keep you warm."

She nuzzled his neck. "Okay. You talked me into it."

"Can't you guys wait until you get to the creek for that?" Jason asked irritably. "I'm trying to concentrate."

Chapter Twelve

Tucker paused on the rise above Colter Creek and listened to the spring thaw rushing past below. This was the highest point for miles around. To the east the moon hung heavy and full. The pale light caught the snowcapped Rocky Mountains stretching along the western horizon. The night air was so cold and clear he could see the lights of Denver as a faint glow in the northwest.

He loved this land. He'd loved it the first time he'd seen it. He felt a part of it in a way he'd never felt a part of anything before.

Until Cassie came into his life.

How was it possible to feel so much a part of her, feel like she was so much a part of him, knowing she planned to leave?

As he gazed at the stars, he heard the crunch of boots. He glanced over his shoulder. Moonlight outlined the slim figure approaching.

Cassie. His woman.

The possessiveness of the thought startled him, but suddenly he knew he was right. She was his woman, and would be for the rest of his life—whether she stayed with him or not.

But he was going to do everything in his power to make her stay.

His angel gave him everything he'd ever needed—hope, a sense of purpose, passion, and what surely had to be love. Gifts of immeasurable value. He felt as if it was Christmas every day they spent together.

But if he didn't do something quick, Christmas would end abruptly in three days. She'd already declared she'd taken enough pictures for the ads. That she was still here was a miracle.

Or was it? Did he dare hope that she could be as reluctant to leave as he was for her to go?

When she was a few steps away, Tucker reached a hand toward her. She walked into his embrace without hesitation, wrapping her arms and her warmth around him. He folded her against him and kissed the top of her hair. She felt so right, nestled close. As though she'd always been holding on to him. As though she'd be holding on forever.

She lifted her face and smiled. "Hi."

He kissed her nose. "Hi."

"What are you doing out here?"

"I checked on the horses and stopped to enjoy the view."

She twisted in his arms and gazed at the distant mountains. "It's a beautiful view."

He studied her lovely features, washed pale by the moonlight. "Yep."

She must have felt his gaze, because she turned her head to find him looking at her. "I was talking about the mountains."

"What mountains?"

She grinned. "Are all cowboys as smooth-talking as you?"

He pulled her back against his chest and rested his chin on her head. "Don't know. I've never been courted by a cowboy."

Instead of chuckling at his joke, she went still. "Is that what you're doing?"

"You mean, you can't tell? I must be slipping."

"Tucker..."

"I know. You're leaving in three days." He tightened his hold. "Tell me. What do we do after that?"

"What do you mean, what do we do? We do what we did before."

"You mean I should act like I never met you? Just blow the whole thing off?" He lowered his voice to a whisper. "Forget that I've kissed an angel?"

She shivered. "I'm not an angel. I'm a woman. A woman who lives two thousand miles away. A woman with a very different life-style. A woman who doesn't fit into your life."

"How do you know how well you fit until you've tried?"

She pulled out of his arms and faced him. "What are you saying?"

"Stay."

She caught a sharp breath. The moonlight behind him showed her changing expressions—from surprise to hope to dismay.

"You want me to stay with you? To give up my life for a man I've known only a few weeks?"

"What does time have to do with anything?" He caught her hand and pulled it against his chest. "As far as your career goes, can't you take pictures out here? You've won so many awards those hot-shot New York agencies will find you wherever you are."

"What about Jason? I'd be acting just like my mother. I have to give him a stable home. He needs it, and he deserves it."

"Jason loves it here. He's grown more as a man in the last five days than all the time he's spent in New York. And as far as being stable, this ranch isn't going anywhere, and neither am I."

"Oh, Tucker. You don't know how much I want to say yes, but I—" The moonlight caught the glint of unshed tears in her eyes. "I'm scared."

"I know, Angel." He pulled her against him. "You don't

need to say anything now. We've got three more days. Just promise you'll think about it. Talk to Jason about staying. See what he thinks. Will you do that?''

She stared up at him a moment, then leaned her head against his chest. ''We've never proven this isn't just physical. What if I moved out here, and we found out that's all it is?''

''This has gone way beyond sex and you know it.''

''I don't know anything anymore,'' Cassie cried softly. ''I'm more confused now than I've ever been in my life.''

Tucker smiled against her hair. ''Good.''

She lifted her head. ''Good? Are you crazy? I used to know exactly what I wanted to do, where I wanted to be.''

''It may not be good for you, but it's good for me because it means I'm getting to you.'' He couldn't resist tasting her lips. ''Just think about it.''

''You're asking me to make a decision about the rest of my life in three days. How can I do that? I need to get to know you better, you need to get to know me.''

''How can we get to know each other when we're thousands of miles apart? We've spent the last two weeks in each other's pockets. And though we gave it our best shot, we haven't been able to do much more than talk. So we know we're compatible outside the bedroom. You know me, Cassie. This is who I am. And I believe I know you. One thing I'm absolutely certain of is, I want you.''

''You want me,'' she repeated.

''More than I've ever wanted anything in my entire life. And you want me, too. Don't you?''

Her eyes dropped. ''Yes, but...''

''But what?''

She sighed. ''Wanting is the language of lust, not love.''

He gently lifted her chin so he could see her face. ''You want me to say I love you. I think I do, but I've never been in love so how can I say for sure? I know I want to be with you every minute of every day. I know the sun shines brighter when we're together. I know the thought of you leaving feels like a knife in my gut. If that isn't love, what is?''

Tears once again shone in her eyes, and she whispered, ''But how do you know those feelings will last?''

He grinned. ''We've already discussed how stubborn I am. Can you see me ever changing my mind?''

''It happens.''

''Not to everyone. Look at Roy and Eileen. Angel, you're a drug that has bonded to every cell in my body. But you're one addiction I don't want to be cured of. The high you give me is natural, and it feels so good. Withdrawal would kill me.''

Cassie slowly ran a finger down the stubble on his cheek. ''Oh, Tucker.''

He gently squeezed her waist. ''Just say you'll think about it, and I'll spend the next three days convincing you.''

''Okay, I'll think about it.'' She wrapped her arms around his neck and pulled his lips down to hers. ''I probably won't be able to think about anything else.''

A low conversation nearby brought Cassie awake. She'd snuggled deep in her bedroll to escape the cold night air. When she felt Tucker stir from the bedroll beside hers, she emerged from her cocoon of thick blankets to find him tugging on his boots. The light of a dancing fire showed his grim features.

Glen's shadow moved against the fire.

''What's wrong?'' she murmured, still fuzzy from sleep.

''Just a little problem Glen and I have to take care of. Go back to sleep. We'll handle it.''

The tightness of his voice cleared her head. ''What is it?''

Glen knelt beside him. ''Best hurry, boss. I don't know how long the boy can hold still.''

Cassie sat up in alarm. ''Boy? What boy?''

''Sssshhhh!'' they hissed at her.

Tucker wrapped his arms around her and said quietly, ''I

was hoping you'd stay asleep. I'll tell you, but whatever you do, don't scream. Okay?''

Her heartbeat accelerated. "What is it?"

"It's Jason. A snake crawled onto his bedroll during the night."

"Jason!" Cassie tried to jump up but Tucker held her down.

"The worst thing you can do—the worst possible thing—is to go screaming over there. A cornered snake is a snake that'll strike. Glen and I will handle it. I want you to stay right here. Understand?''

"But—"

"No buts, Cassie. If I don't have your word on this, I'm going to have J.C. hold you down with his hand over your mouth. Jason needs to stay calm. He's doing great so far, but if he sees your fear, it'll trigger his."

She tried to take a deep breath, but air didn't want to enter her lungs. So she nodded.

He gave her a quick, hard kiss, then rose. He didn't bother putting on his jacket, though the air had a bite that made Cassie reach for hers as she watched Tucker, J.C. and Glen confer by the fire. Her heart thudded with dread.

Jason had gone to sleep on the opposite side of the blaze beside Jimmy, but Cassie couldn't see him because of the flames Glen or J.C. had built up. Very quietly, very slowly, she crept to the right until she could see her brother's form outlined by a green army blanket. He lay on his side, perfectly still, a thick, dark coil lay in the curve of his body.

A whimper escaped. To keep from racing over to save her brother, she pulled her knees into her chest and wrapped her arms around them.

As she watched, unable to breathe, the three men split up. Tucker held back as Glen and J.C. quietly moved to the left, into the darkness beyond the firelight. Her eyes followed their indistinct shadows as they circled around, quiet as the wind.

Finally Tucker began to move. Though he'd demanded she be quiet, he scuffed and shuffled his way around the fire until a triangular head rose from the coils beside her brother. As Tucker slowly moved closer, Cassie heard a distinct rattling.

To keep from screaming, she planted her mouth against her knee.

What made everything worse was knowing she couldn't do anything to protect her brother. She hated being helpless. Hated having to depend on these men to save her brother's life.

Her mind caught on the word "depend."

She was depending on Tucker—a man she'd known only a few weeks. Because she wanted him, she'd put her brother in danger. Now she was sitting by—helpless—both of them at the mercy of a man who was practically a stranger.

What's worse—she'd done it over and over. First the ravine, then the manure, now this.

How was she any different from her mother?

The closer Tucker got to the snake, the louder and faster it rattled, the higher it lifted its ugly head. What was he doing?

A movement in the shadows caught Cassie's attention. It was Glen, easing his way up behind Jason.

The plan became horribly, sickeningly obvious. Tucker would distract the snake until Glen grabbed it from behind.

Tucker was putting himself in danger for Jason.

At that moment, Cassie knew for certain that she loved this cowboy.

She also knew she couldn't stay.

She'd thought she might be over her obsessive need for independence. Now she knew she wasn't. The obsession went far deeper than she'd realized. It was who she was.

The thought saddened her, but also brought comfort. Her need for independence was familiar, something she could wrap her mind around to get her through the horror of the moment.

Her eyes shifted from Tucker to Glen to her brother's still form.

Don't move, Jason. We may have to depend on these men now, but I promise you, we never will again.

Tucker knelt a few feet from the snake. Hatless, he kept his eyes on the reptile. The snake concentrated on Tucker, seemingly oblivious to the hand inching its way across Jason.

Glen's hand crept closer and closer.

Cassie couldn't breathe.

The fact that the snake now had more pressing targets to strike than her brother didn't comfort her. How could Glen grab the snake without it biting him? How long could Tucker stare at the snake without being struck?

Cassie jerked when the snake suddenly bared its fangs, but Tucker didn't move a muscle. Just when Cassie thought she couldn't sit still another second, Glen's hand shot out and grabbed the snake just below the head.

"Got him!" Glen lifted a hissing, thrashing snake high in the air.

Suddenly the whole camp came alive. Jimmy and Mike sat up, with J.C. right behind them. Both boys exclaimed their excitement. Tucker stood in obvious relief and glanced over at her.

The only one who didn't move was Jason.

What was wrong? Had the snake bitten him before anyone knew?

Cassie tried to rush to him, but her muscles had been clenched so hard so long it took several seconds to unbend them.

By that time, Tucker noticed Jason's stillness. The cowboy reached down and tried to peel back his bedroll, but Jason held tight to the blankets as everyone gathered around him.

"What is it, Jason?" Cassie lurched to the other side of the fire. "Are you hurt? Get up. Please!"

Jason shook his head wildly, refusing to meet her eyes, but she could see tears of fright and rage in his.

Tucker knelt beside him. "It's over, Tick. You did real good. I'm proud of you."

"You want to look at this thing before I get shed of it?" Glen asked. "It sure is a whopper."

Cassie glanced at the snake and shivered. It was as thick as Glen's arm and nearly touched the ground when it wasn't writhing around the cowboy. How could he stand there, holding it so calmly?

"Are you going to kill it?" she asked.

"Not unless you want it for a souvenir." He grabbed the tail and held the snake out. "Make a nice belt."

"No!" Jason cried. "Get rid of it. I don't ever want to see it again."

"Can't say as I blame you. The boss was right, Tick. You done real good. Stayed calm and still. There's not many that'd have done half so good." With that praise the cowboy turned and walked down the hill.

"Can we go home?" Jason asked feveredly.

"Not until you get up." Tucker flipped away the blankets to reveal a dark stain on Jason's pants.

Mike snickered. "Look, it scared the pee out of him!"

Jason went white and turned his back on the group gathered above him.

Cassie quickly covered her brother as J.C. cuffed Mike on the shoulder for his thoughtless remark.

"You get on outta here, boy," the cowboy said harshly. "Roy'll deal with you later."

"Yeah, you'd a been swimming in pee if it had happened to you," Jimmy told the red-faced boy as Mike went past him.

"Hell, I probably would'a, too," J.C. drawled. "Com'on, Jimmy. Let's start breakfast."

They moved away, leaving just the three of them.

"Don't worry about it, Tick," Tucker said quietly. "It happens to everybody."

"I hate it here. I want to go home."

Cassie knew at once that Jason was talking about New York, not the ranch house.

Relief sank into her bones. Her brother had just provided her with the perfect excuse to leave. Her independence—and her heart along with it—was safe.

"Cassie?" Jason whined.

"We'll be on our way just as soon as we eat and pack up," Tucker said.

"Not your home. Mine." The boy turned pleading eyes her way. "Please, Cassie. I just want to go home."

"Put your coat on," she told him. "I'll pack our things."

Tucker threw a narrow-eyed glance between them. "Breakfast will be ready soon."

"I'm not hungry." Jason sat up and slipped into the old sheepskin-lined jacket of Tucker's. It reached mid-thigh, covering the embarrassing stain.

Tucker grabbed his arm. "Jason, you can't just—"

Jason flung him off and stood. "I'll saddle our horses, Cassie."

Tucker turned to her. "You can't go until we're packed." He ran a hand down her arm. "Jason has been in a state close to shock. He needs something to eat. So do you."

"I'm not hungry, either."

"Cassie, he'll be okay. It was just a snake."

"Just a snake? No. 'Just a snake' is seeing one crawling several yards away, not waking up with one curled up on your chest." She pulled away from his touch. "He could've been killed."

"Not likely. That old diamondback was too cold to strike anything quickly. That's why he crawled onto Jason—for warmth. Even if Tick had been bitten, we always carry anti-venom in the first-aid kit."

All Cassie could see were those deadly fangs. All she could feel was her utter helplessness during that awful moment. "He could've died."

"Cassie, this was a fluke. Glen's seen it before, but I've never seen a snake do this. I can just about guarantee it'll never happen to Jason again."

She squared her shoulders. "I can guarantee it."

His eyes narrowed. "What do you mean?"

She sighed and pushed to her feet. "I have to see about Jason."

He stood and grabbed her arm. "What do you mean, you can guarantee it?"

"Let me go, Tucker," she said softly. "He's my brother."

"And what am I?"

She searched his eyes in the growing light of dawn. She knew what he was asking. What she was doing to him—and to herself—cut deep. Like a razor-sharp stiletto. That the wound was self-inflicted didn't make it hurt any less. As it was, the pain nearly brought her to her knees.

She knew exactly what she was slicing out of her life—the love of a lifetime. But she also knew she had to do it. For Jason. And for herself.

"You're in my way," she said, then walked deliberately around him.

Tucker told J.C. to forget about breakfast, then they packed the gear and all headed to the house together.

Tucker didn't try to ride close to Cassie on the way back. He knew she didn't mean what she'd said to him. She was in shock. She needed time to think, to calm down, to realize this was just a minor incident in the life of a boy.

Jason had stuck close by her side and when they reached the house, both of them went upstairs.

Tucker gave them half an hour to get showered and changed, then he knocked on Jason's door.

"Who is it?" Jason called stiffly.

"Tucker."

"What do you want?"

Tucker eased the door open. Jason was alone in the room, his suitcase open on his bed.

Tucker's heart skidded to a halt. "You're packing."

"Duh."

The boy's animosity was as palpable as it had been the day they'd met in New York. The boy had had a scare that morn-

ing, but Tucker would've bet real money it'd take more than
a snake to make the boy run away. Now he realized he
would've lost the bet.

What else was he going to lose?

"Where's Cassie?"

Jason wouldn't meet his eyes. "She's packing, too."

Tucker closed Jason's door, then strode down to Cassie's,
which was open. She was kneeling by an open drawer of the
chest, pulling out clothes. Tucker entered without knocking
and closed the door behind him.

"You aren't taking Tick seriously? You can't leave because
of a teenage temper tantrum."

She hesitated, but didn't look at him. "Yes, I can. I have
to."

"Last night you promised you'd think about staying."

"I did think about it, all the way back from camp. There's
no way, Tucker. We don't belong here."

Tucker felt as if his heart were being ripped from his chest.
"You're supposed to stay until Sunday. Is two more days so
much to ask?"

"Yes." Her voice sounded dead.

He took three long strides across the room, grabbed her
arms and hauled her to her feet. Clothes fell to the floor, but
he didn't give a damn. "Why?"

She fought his hold, and he let her go. She backed up several steps and glared at him. "He could've been killed."

"Even if Jason had been bitten, he wouldn't have died. I
told you, we carry antivenom in the first-aid kit. The worst
that would've happened is he might've gotten sick." Tucker
drove a hand back through his hair. "You can't tell me he's
not in danger in New York. Drivers there would as soon run
you down as look at you. Hell, you can die from the fumes
alone. And people get mugged night and day."

"That's true. But we understand the rules in New York. It's
our home."

She said those last words with emphasis. They felt like daggers.

"Jason has made friends in New York," she continued. "Friends who don't laugh at him for every little thing he does wrong."

"That's because he doesn't do anything except what he's already good at—computer games. He doesn't have anything to challenge him there. When he does find something challenging he loves it, until he makes a mistake. Then he runs away—just like you." He took a step closer. "But that's the only thing you know how to teach him, isn't it? Running. You learned it at your mother's knee."

Her eyes narrowed, and she clenched her fists as if she could barely keep from slapping him. "This is about Jason, not my mother."

"The hell it is." Tucker knew he was pushing her, but it was the only option he had left. He needed to make her see what she was doing to Jason...and to him. "Eight husbands couldn't have been all bad luck, Angel. All this time you've thought the men ran out on your mother. What if it was the other way around?"

Cassie swallowed hard. "You don't know a damn thing about my mother."

"No, but her daughter runs when she starts to get close to somebody. And now I see her son does, too. Where else would both you and Jason have learned that trait?"

"I don't know how you can suggest my mother ran because she was afraid of getting close. She married all those men. You can't get any closer than that."

"I don't know the reasons your mother left all those husbands, but I know why you're leaving me. You're falling in love with me, and it scares you to death."

Cassie winced, but didn't look away. "Men come and go, but Jason will be my brother for the rest of our lives. In New York, he'll have a stable life, with a good school, friends and me. I can't take him away from that on the off chance our relationship will work. I've known too many that have failed. You say I run away like my mother. You may be right. But there's one way I'm not like her—I refuse to shuffle Jason from home to home just because I think I've fallen in love. He deserves a better life than that, and I intend to give it to him."

Tucker felt as though he'd been hit up the side of the head with a two-by-four. He'd never even had a chance. Cassie intended to be the mother to Jason that her mother never was—no matter what it cost her personally.

"What about you, Cassie? What do you deserve?"

"I deserve to be left alone to do what I need to do." She lifted her stubborn chin. "Jason is not your son, Tucker. He's not your responsibility. I have to do what I think is right for him. Can't you understand?"

Tucker did understand, all too well. He felt as if he were back in foster care. Another family he thought he was a part of was being ripped away.

Suddenly he knew without a doubt. He loved this woman. And he loved this boy. But he had absolutely no rights where either one of them was concerned.

Who needs you?

Obviously, no one.

The same pride that kept him going all those years in foster homes resurfaced. He'd never begged for love from anyone, and he'd be damned if he'd start now.

He wheeled around and headed out the door. "I'll have one of the men drive you to the airport."

"Tucker, wait..."

He stopped at the door and looked over his shoulder. "For what?"

She didn't reply, though she looked as if she wanted to, so he prodded. "What do you need, Cassie?"

She shook her head and turned away. "Nothing."

The word ripped through him, tearing his heart from his chest.

He shut the door behind him.

Chapter Thirteen

A week later, Cassie spread the transparencies across the light table, then forced her hand to the switch.

Turn it on, Cassie. Erica's going to be here in two hours. You've got to look at these damn photos. You've been putting it off for a week. You can't avoid it any longer.

She took a deep breath and flipped the switch. A hundred Tuckers stared up at her. A hundred pairs of neon-blue eyes. A hundred sexy smiles. Thank God, they were only as big as her thumb.

She had to select ten of the best shots. This was her job, damn it. Surely she could look at them objectively.

She grabbed the magnifying glass and ran it slowly across the rows, culling photo after photo. An hour later, only ten remained. She slid them into the special presentation sleeve she'd already prepared, then slipped the sleeve into a Burch Photography envelope and labeled it.

When she turned back to the rejected photos spread across the light table, she wrapped the excess of her faded sweatshirt around her and stared. Moments frozen in time. She remembered each one vividly—J.C. teasing Tucker as she took the ones beside the barn, Tucker's horse walking up and knocking off his hat just as she shot the photos on the ridge, the sexy things he said to her as she focused on him there by the fire.

How had she found the strength to leave this man? She missed him so much she felt physical pain. She couldn't eat, she couldn't sleep, and she could only perform the most rudimentary tasks of her job, like developing film. Two weeks ago she'd been perfectly happy living alone. Now there was a hole in her life the size of...

The size of a six-foot-two, hundred-ninety pound cowboy.

She loved him. There was no doubt of it now—now that it was too late. Now she would never be the center of anyone's universe, because Tucker was the only man she would ever love...and she would never see him again.

She had her independence, but for the first time, independence didn't make her happy.

With cold, trembling fingers, she carefully slid the rejected transparencies back in the envelope and placed it in the filing cabinet under "R" for Richman Cosmetics. As she closed the drawer she felt as if she was extinguishing all the light and warmth in the cosmos.

Tucker walked into the kitchen and dropped an odd-shaped leather bag onto the counter.

Eileen sat at the kitchen table, nursing a cup of coffee. "What's that?"

"Some kind of equipment of Cassie's. I found it in the office." He felt his face tighten as her name left his lips. It was the first time he'd said it out loud since she'd walked out a week ago, leaving him to pick up the pieces of his heart. "Pack it up and mail it to her, would you?"

"Don't have her address," the old woman told him, her eyes narrowed.

Cussing under his breath, Tucker grabbed a pen from the jar on the table and a napkin and scribbled the New York address. "There."

"Why don't you take it to the post office yourself? You're heading north in a couple of days, ain't you?"

He straightened. "How'd you know that?"

"Your traveling buddy Clay Hicks called 'bout an hour ago. Said for you to pick him up Thursday at the airport in Billings." Her lips pursed as if she were sucking on a lime.

"Thanks."

"So you ain't gonna listen to that doctor?"

"Bull riding's what I do, Eileen."

The old woman snorted. "Never did know a cowboy who had a nickel's worth of sense about their health. I've seen 'em work with broken arms, broken legs, broken heads, just about anything that could be broke. Thought you had more sense."

Tucker turned his gaze out the kitchen window. He knew the risk he was taking, returning to rodeo. The truth was, he just didn't care. In fact, he hoped like hell a bull would kick him so hard Cassie would fly right out of his head.

As if she could read his mind, Eileen said, "Them bulls can't knock her outta your heart, Tucker."

Tucker felt his jaw stiffen. Eileen might be right, but that didn't mean he couldn't let them try.

Eileen sighed. "Cassie's phone number around anywhere?"

"Why?"

"Thought I might let her know a package is coming...and one is going."

"It's none of her business if I get back on a bull. She made her choice."

"From what I heard, sounds like Jason made the choice, and she didn't have enough gumption to tell the boy no."

"What makes you think she'll find any gumption now?"

"Our Cassie's not stupid. She'll figger out she's not doing that boy any good by letting him have his way all the time. Especially when it comes to something she wants as bad as she wants you."

Despite his efforts to shield himself, hope speared through

Tucker, bursting through the thin veneer of protection he'd built around his shattered heart.

Would Cassie care if he climbed onto the back of another bull? She'd made him promise not to rodeo, and he told her he wouldn't—as long as she stayed. Would she come back if she knew, to keep him from riding? Or would Jason keep her in New York forever?

Tucker rubbed his jaw. Tick. If there was any hope of getting Cassie back to Colorado, her brother was the key. Tucker was certain Jason liked the ranch, would love living here. If only he could convince the boy to give it another try.

He spun on his heel and headed out of the kitchen.

"Where you going?" Eileen asked.

"Into the office to work on the computer." He stopped and smiled for the first time since Cassie left. "The best way to catch an angel is with a 'Net."

Two nights later Cassie turned over in bed for the fifty-third time that night. She'd counted.

This was ridiculous. She needed sleep. An account exec from a new agency was coming in tomorrow to discuss a job—which was both good and bad. She was looking forward to having work to occupy her mind, but she'd have to dress like a professional for the first time since they returned.

Cassie glanced at the clock and sighed. Two forty-eight. Might as well get up. She wasn't accomplishing anything in bed.

She pulled on her favorite sweats, grabbed a soft drink from the refrigerator and entered her studio. The black walls and still air echoed the way she felt inside—dead. With a tiny shiver, she hurried into her office and switched on the computer. Light flared into the room with a satisfying ding.

Might as well check her e-mail. A virtual life was better than no life at all.

She pulled her chair over and logged onto the Internet service. An animated voice welcomed her, then told her she had mail. A moment later she blinked as she saw the list of letters scrolling across the screen.

She had sixteen letters? She only used the service for an e-mail address for the studio. She'd never had so many letters.

Then she realized why. Jason had used the computer that afternoon while she did inventory on her film. She'd forgotten and hadn't changed the user name when she'd logged on. This was Jason's mail. He "talked" to people all over the world.

But wait a minute. She didn't know Jason's password.

She smiled then as she realized they both used the same one—the name of a dog they'd had when Jason was little. She was just about to log off when a window suddenly popped onto the screen with a "bling."

What the heck? Someone thought Jason was on-line and was sending him an instant message. Intrigued, she leaned closer. She'd never seen one be—

Suddenly she recognized the screen name of the sender. CLazy7. Circle Lazy Seven. Tucker.

Unable to move, her heart pounding against her rib cage, she read the message.

CLAZY7: Finally caught you on-line, like you asked. What the hell are you doing up at this hour?

Panic swept through Cassie. Tucker thought he was talking to Jason. What should she do? It sounded as though Jason had contacted Tucker first. But why? She thought her brother hated the ranch and everyone on it.

CLAZY7: You there, Tick?

Tucker was waiting for a response. She couldn't let him know she was the one receiving his message. She was too raw to talk to him. But...

She wanted to hear his voice, even if it was just electronically, even if he thought he was talking to Jason. She'd answer him, then make some excuse about thunderstorms and log off.

So, what would Jason's reply be?

Hesitantly, she placed her fingers over the keys and typed, "Can't sleep."

As she clicked on the Send button, Jason's screen name— he'd evidently changed it to Tick—appeared in front of her comment.

CLAZY7: I can't answer your question any way you're going to like it. The boys who live on the ranch don't have any family at all…

She had plenty of time to read the first line two times before the second appeared on the screen. Tucker was not the fastest typist.

CLAZY7: They're too wild for the system to handle, so Roy takes a crack at them. I'm sorry, but you can't come live at the ranch by yourself. You belong with your sister.
    Cassie loves you more than anything else in the world. Believe me. I know.

So many emotions swept through Cassie, one right on top of another, it took several minutes to sort through them.

Jason obviously wanted to live on Tucker's ranch. Why couldn't he have told her?

She'd given up a lot to make her brother happy. Seemed as if she couldn't do anything right when it came to Jason. Would she ever understand him? Would she ever know what he needed? The way Tucker seemed to know?

Tucker.

Emotions tumbled through her. She'd never loved her cowboy more than she did right now. She'd kicked him in the teeth. He had every right to be bitter. When most people split up, they break relations off with every member of their previous partner's family, but Tucker still had time to reason with a confused teenage boy. He seemed to genuinely care for Jason. And he had enough class to say nice things about her.

This was not the kind of man who would run away at the first sign of trouble. This was a man she could count on…forever.

Cassie blinked away tears and touched the computer screen, as if she could feel the rasp of Tucker's five o'clock shadow across the miles.

CLAZY7: Tick? You there?

Tucker was waiting for a response—from Jason. What would Jason reply? It would help if she knew what he'd asked in the first place.

TICK: I'm here.

CLAZY7: You're not upset, are you?

Upset? Of course she was upset. And evidently Jason was upset. Wasn't Tucker?

TICK: What about you? Aren't you upset? I thought you and Cassie liked each other.

There was a moment's pause, then:

CLAZY7: I thought so, too. But things didn't work out. I tried to get her to move out here with you, but she left because you wanted to.

Cassie hesitated. Would Jason ask the question she was burning to ask Tucker?

Then she smiled. Jason was thirteen. He'd ask anything.

TICK: Do you hate her now? What if she changed her mind?

CLAZY7: How can I hate her when I love her so much? If you want to come back, I'll welcome you both with arms stretched from one end of the Rockies to the other.

He loved her. The words were strong and simple. Just like Tucker. Was he certain? She placed her hands on the keys to ask but had to read his continued message first.

CLAZY7: I love you, too, Tick. Come visit when you can. We can always use a top hand around here. I've got to go now. Got a date Friday night with Twist N Shout.

Cassie's pulse slowed when she saw the word "date" roll across the screen, but the name made her heart stop. "Twist N Shout" sounded like a bull.

TICK: Who the hell is Twist N Shout?

CLAZY7: A bull in Calgary. That's in Canada, in case you didn't know.

Cassie stared at the screen in horror. She'd seen him ride a bull twice, and both times he'd ended up in the hospital. This time he'd probably kill himself.
She couldn't type fast enough.

TICK: No, Tucker!!!!! You can't ride bulls anymore. You promised!!!

Nearly two thousand miles away, Tucker stared at his computer screen. Jason didn't know he wasn't supposed to ride bulls. The only ones who knew were Eileen and...

Cassie.

His heart—the one he'd thought broken beyond repair—thudded loudly in his chest. Somehow Cassie had logged on under Jason's screen name.

Tucker cussed as he realized he'd ruined all of Jason's neat plans for secrecy. The boy didn't want Cassie to know yet that he wanted to live on the ranch, though Tucker had been trying to talk him into telling her for two days.

Tucker cussed again. To hell with what Jason wanted. Eileen was right. The boy had gotten his way once too often. It was time Cassie knew the truth.

Then Cassie's comments sank in, and happiness swept over Tucker like a spring flood. She was worried. If she didn't love him, she wouldn't give a damn if he killed himself.

CLAZY7: Cassie?

When he got no reply, he typed: "Cassie? That you?"
A window popped onto his screen.

TICK is not currently signed on.

Tucker leaned back in his chair. So she'd run away...again.

He reached for the phone, determined to call her and tell her to pack their bags, that he was coming to New York to get them.

But before his hand picked up the receiver, he stopped.

No. He had to let Cassie make the decision. She had to realize that she loved him enough to trust him not to take away her independence.

He glanced at the clock. He'd give her forty-eight hours to figure it out.

He'd never wanted anything in his life as bad as he wanted Cassie—not even his gold buckles. She was just going to have to get over her fears that he'd desert her the way she thought all her stepfathers deserted her mother. He was going to love her for the rest of his life. He deserved her, he'd worked hard to win her, and by damn, he was going to have her.

In the meantime, he was going to give her a scare.

He rose to gather the things he'd need for his drive to Canada.

Cassie shoved back from the computer, her wide eyes never leaving the screen as her chair rolled halfway across the office. *Stupid, stupid, stupid.*

For two seconds, she forgot to be Jason. Now Tucker knew.

As her pulse began to slow, she considered that. What did he know? Since the Instant Message window had remained on the screen, she reviewed the "conversation."

The only thing Tucker knew for sure was she went ballistic when he told her he was going to another rodeo. But that probably meant he knew—or at least suspected—that she loved him.

Cassie sat back in her chair, relief and hope washing through her.

So? She did love him. She wanted to be with him for the rest of her life. And it sounded as though Jason wanted to live at the ranch, too.

Jason. Why didn't he tell her? And why had she listened to him when he'd insisted on leaving? Tucker knew it was just a teenage tantrum that Jason would be sorry for. Why didn't she?

Because she had absolutely no experience raising teenage boys.

But Tucker did. Jason needed Tucker.

And so did she. Being independent without Tucker was far worse than being dependent on him.

Her need for independence had been driven by necessity. Since her mother had forced her—through sheer neglect—to take care of herself at an early age, Cassie had made a religion out of it.

No man is an island. Who said that? Whoever it was, he or

she was right. People needed people. Jason needed her. She needed Tucker. And Tucker seemed to need her, too.

Love was not the prison her mother had made of it. She didn't feel caged by Tucker's love. In fact, when she was with him, she felt freer than she'd ever felt in her life.

Her gaze dropped to the telephone. Cassie knew Tucker was awake, and alone in that big, empty house.

She reached for the receiver, but stopped before she picked it up. It wasn't cowardice this time, though. First she needed to have a little talk with a certain brother of hers. What they had here was a failure to communicate. But that was about to be fixed, even if it was three o'clock in the morning.

She shut down the computer, made her way to Jason's door and rapped loudly.

"Yeah?" The answer came immediately.

Cassie pushed the panel open. Her brother lay stretched out under the uncurtained window, dimly lit by city lights. "You're not sleeping, either."

"No."

She sat on the edge of his mattress. "Want to talk about it?"

Though his face was shadowed, she could tell he watched her warily. "Talk about what?"

"About why you want to live at the Circle Lazy Seven." She cleared her throat, but it didn't clear the pain from her voice. "I thought you wanted to live with me."

"Oh, jeez, Cassie, of course I do!" He sat up and reached for her, though he stopped short of touching. "I just... I never thought about how you'd feel. I'm sorry. I didn't think there'd be a chance, but I had to ask. How'd you find out? Did Tucker call you?"

She shook her head. "I logged on under your password by mistake. He sent me—you an instant message."

"What did he say?"

She laid a hand on his arm. "That the boys who live with Roy and Eileen need a home a whole lot worse than you, but you were welcome to visit anytime. He said the ranch can always use one more top hand.''

Jason brightened. "He used those words? Top hand?"

She nodded. "Is that good?"

"Only the best cowboys are called top hands."

One more reason to love Tucker. "Why do you want to live on the ranch? Because of Tucker?"

"Some, I guess. But it's different there than anywhere I've ever lived. There was stuff to do all the time with the horses or the cows or the cowboys. Stuff that really meant something."

"What about sliding down the ravine, and the manure, and the snake?"

"Well, sliding down the ravine was just plain stupid, but I've learned that lesson. And the manure wasn't so bad. Besides, Eileen told me they do that to all the new cowboys. And I've been doing snake research on the Internet since we got back. Did you know that snakes are cowards first, bluffers second and only strike if there's no other way out? Most snakes, anyway. And they're cold-blooded. That's why that old snake crawled up on me. He just wanted to get warm." He hesitantly touched her hand. "I'm sorry, Cassie."

Cassie took his hand between hers. "Sorry about what?"

"Sorry I made you leave. Tucker and me have been e-mailing each other for a couple of days. That's why I had enough courage to ask him if I could go back. It sounds like he misses you real bad. I've been meaning to tell you I want to go back, but I was the one that made us leave and all. I figured being stuck in New York was my punishment for being such a stupid baby about that snake."

Cassie squeezed his hand. "You weren't a baby. You were very brave to be still long enough for Tucker and Glen to help you. I was proud of you. Tucker was, too, you know."

"Yeah, I know. Anyway, from now on I'm going to think things through before I react like a kid."

She pulled him into her arms. "You're growing up into a fine young man. I love you so much."

"You...love me?"

She hugged him harder. "Of course I love you. You're my brother. I should've told you a long time ago. I should tell you every day. I'm sorry. I'll do better from now on."

He wrapped his arms around her. She heard tears in his voice as he said, "I love you, too, Cassie. I always have. If things got bad around the house, I knew I could call you and you'd make me feel better."

"Oh, Jason, we've both got a lot to learn." She pulled away and smoothed his hair back from his forehead. "But I know who can help us. Tucker."

He stared at her with wide eyes. "You mean it? You don't hate him?"

"No. I love him, Jason. Think you'd mind adding him to our family?"

"Are you kidding? When? Can we go tomorrow?"

She chuckled. "You have school tomorrow."

"Aw, I can go to school out there."

"We can't move overnight, you know. Think of all my equipment." She sighed. "Besides, tomorrow I have to cancel an appointment I have with a new agency, then fly to Canada and drag Tucker's butt off a bull."

"Huh? Why?"

"A doctor told Tucker not to ride bulls anymore. He's had too many concussions."

"I've heard about that. A lot of football players and boxers and stuff get their brains scrambled that way."

"Yes, well, I don't know about them, but I do know about a certain cowboy. Think you can spend a couple of nights with Sam?"

"Sure." Jason grinned. "Go get 'im, Cassie!"

Tucker wrapped the leather string around the wrist of his bull riding glove and pulled the knot tight with his teeth. He felt behind his thighs to make sure his chaps were securely buckled, then climbed over the chute rail on top of the gray Brahman bull named Twist N Shout. He settled his bull rope against the bull's hump, then held it in position as Clay reached underneath the belly to grab the end.

The routine was as familiar to him as brushing his teeth and, for the first time in his life, about as exciting.

Cassie hadn't come to save him from the big bad bull.

Maybe he was expecting too much. Calgary was a long way from New York City. Maybe she had work to do. Maybe she didn't have anyone to leave Jason with. Maybe…

Maybe she just doesn't need you.

"You okay, Tuck?" Clay asked as he handed Tucker the tail of the bull rope. "You ain't said ten words since you picked me up in Montana."

"Shut up, Clay. I'm in the zone."

"You ain't in no zone, neither. That's why I'm worried. What's the matter? New York get to you?"

"Yeah, Clay. New York got to me." Tucker wrapped the tail of the bull rope around his resined glove.

"You're up next, Tucker. Soon as you're ready," the chute boss said from the arena floor. "Hey, what's going on over there?"

Tucker ignored the cowboys gawking at a commotion near the participants' entrance as well as the cheers of the arena crowd when his name was announced. He took a deep breath and tried to will himself into that place in his mind that made riding bulls like riding a tricycle. But it wouldn't come. All he could think about was—

"Tucker, you promised!"

The strident voice was an angel choir, direct from heaven. He grinned. Cassie came. She loved him. She *needed* him. Thank God.

He unwrapped the bull rope, then braced his hands on the rails on either side of the chute.

"Cowboy up!" the chute boss called. "Hey, Tucker, where you going? You're up next."

Tucker lifted himself off the bull. "Sorry, Chester. I'm drawing out."

"What?"

"You heard me."

Tucker stepped onto the platform. It felt strange. This was something he'd never done. Once he climbed on a bull, the only way he'd ever gotten off was landing in the dirt, one way or another.

"I'm drawing out, boys," Tucker announced to the crowd behind the chutes. "My rodeoing days are over. Now let me through."

"Where you going, Tuck?" another bull rider asked.

"I've got a date with an angel," he replied as he pushed his way along the platform. He ignored the questions and comments around him, the amazement that for the first time since he'd joined the Professional Rodeo Cowboys Association, Tucker Reeves refused to ride his bull.

As he moved down the platform, he spied Cassie arguing with the guard at the entrance. Only participants and other officials were allowed behind the chutes.

She was laying it on Henry hot and heavy, but the old cowboy had dug in. He'd dealt with too many buckle bunnies trying to cuddle up to bull and bronc riders to let a female enter the male domain behind the rough stock chutes.

As Tucker descended the steps, Cassie spied him. She waved frantically. "Tucker! Over here! Thank God you got off that bull. Will you please tell this…this cowboy to let me in?"

Tucker stopped several yards short of the entrance. He propped his fists on his hips and battled to keep a stupid grin from his face. "Hell, no."

She blinked hard. "But, Tucker, I came all this way to…"

"To what?" he demanded.

She glanced around. Every cowboy within hearing distance

watched them. But Tucker didn't care. If he let her in she'd be in his arms in two seconds flat, and they had a few things they had to get straight first.

Cassie hedged. "To talk to you."

"So, talk."

"Come here, then, if they won't let me in."

"Nope."

Her face screwed into a grimace of frustration. "You want me to tell you I love you in front of everybody?"

Joy unlike he'd ever known sprang from a dark corner deep inside. It washed over him in waves of healing light. He realized in that instant that nothing he'd done had earned Cassie's love. Her love was a gift—a very precious gift—not a paycheck for work completed.

The realization humbled him...and thrilled him beyond words. He wanted to rush out the gate and yank Cassie into his arms.

But he couldn't. Not yet.

He pushed his hat back on his head and nodded. "In front of God and all these witnesses."

"All right, then," she huffed. "I love you."

"Now say it like you mean it."

She glared at him a minute, then relaxed and smiled. "Come over here, and I'll show you I mean it."

Her statement got them several hoots and colorful suggestions from the cowboys surrounding them.

"I love you, Tucker Reeves," she said in a clear, strong voice. "I think I've loved you since the first time you smiled at me."

He finally let his own smile break through. "I love you, too, Angel."

"Now will you come over here? I need to kiss you."

More catcalls from their audience.

"I need to kiss you, too. But first I want a few questions answered."

"Like what?" she asked suspiciously.

"Like how long are you planning on sticking around this time?"

"As long as you want me."

He took half a step before he caught himself. "I want you forever, Angel. Can you deal with that?"

"It better be forever, cowboy. I never thought I'd say the words, but since I'm going to say them, I'm going to take 'until death do us part' literally. Now will you come here?"

Tucker's grin widened as several cowboys encouraged him to oblige his woman, but he shook his head. "Where you planning on living?"

"With you. Where else would I live?"

"What about your photography?"

"I'm not giving that up. You're going to have to let me go away now and then so I can earn a living."

He nodded. He didn't expect her to give up all her independence. "As long as you come back to me."

"I will. I promise. Now put your bowed legs in motion and come here."

"What about Jason?"

"Tucker!"

"He's coming, too, isn't he?"

"Of course he's coming. We're a package deal."

"I want us to adopt him, Cassie. You told me he isn't my responsibility, but I want him to be. I want to have an official say-so in his raising."

"I'm sure my mother won't object, and Jason will love having you as his sixth and final father." She smiled wryly. "Although I don't know what that will make me."

"We'll work the legal stuff out later."

She nodded. "Any more questions?"

"Just one."

"What now?" she asked, throwing her hands in the air.

"Will you marry me?"

Her face softened, and she searched his eyes for an endless

minute. A hush fell over the crowd around them in anticipation of her answer.

In a low, sexy voice, she said, "Not unless you kiss me this instant."

Tucker took four long strides, vaulted over the gate because he couldn't wait for it to be opened, and took her in his arms. Amid more hoots and hollers and congratulatory slaps on the back, he kissed her.

She melted into him and for a short stretch of eternity, they were oblivious to anything else.

Finally he stepped back. "Now—will you marry me?"

She smiled. "Yes."

He couldn't help tasting her lips again.

"Can we go someplace a little more private?" she whispered in his ear. "I need you."

Tucker went still. "Say it again."

She pulled back far enough to meet his gaze. "What? That I need you?"

He smoothed a strand of hair from her face. "I've waited a lifetime to hear those words. I'm glad they came from you."

She gave him a sexy smile. "Let's get out of here, cowboy, and I'll show you exactly how much I need you."

With a whoop of elation, Tucker picked her up and spun with her in his arms. The cowboys hanging on the back fence cheered.

When he came to a halt, Cassie kissed him. "Have I told you lately that I love you?"

He smiled and held her even tighter. "I love you, too."

Her smile nearly blinded him as she ran a hand lovingly down his jaw. "I know. I'm going to depend on that fact...forever."

He placed his forehead against hers. "Forever, my sweet Christmas angel."

She cocked her head. "It's not anywhere near Christmas."

"That's what you think." He tasted her lips again, then

smiled down at her. "Now that I have my very own bright, shining angel, every day is going to be Christmas...for the rest of our lives."

* * * * *

Look Who's Celebrating Our 20th Anniversary:

"Happy 20th birthday, Silhouette. You made the writing dream of hundreds of women a reality. You enabled us to give [women] the stories [they] wanted to read and helped us teach [them] about the power of love."

—*New York Times* bestselling author
Debbie Macomber

"I wish you continued success, Silhouette Books.... Thank you for giving me a chance to do what I love best in all the world."

—International bestselling author
Diana Palmer

"A visit to Silhouette is a guaranteed happy ending, a chance to touch magic for a little while.... It refreshes and revitalizes and makes us feel better.... I hope Silhouette goes on forever."

—Award-winning bestselling author
Marie Ferrarella

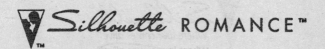

Silhouette ROMANCE™

Celebrate
Silhouette's 20th Anniversary

with *New York Times* bestselling author

LINDA HOWARD

and the long-awaited story of
CHANCE MACKENZIE

in

A GAME OF CHANCE

IM #1021
On sale in August 2000

Hot on the trail of a suspected terrorist, covert intelligence officer Chance Mackenzie found, seduced and subtly convinced the man's daughter, Sunny Miller, to lead her father out of hiding. The plan worked, but then Sunny discovered the truth behind Chance's so-called affections. Now the agent who *always* got his man had to figure out a way to get his woman!

Available at your favorite retail outlet.

Silhouette®
Where love comes alive™

Visit Silhouette at www.eHarlequin.com   SIMCHANCE

ATTENTION,
LINDSAY McKENNA FANS!

Morgan Trayhern has three brand-new missions in Lindsay McKenna's latest series:

Morgan's men are made for battle— but are they ready for love?

The excitement begins in July 2000, with
Lindsay McKenna's 50th book!

MAN OF PASSION
(Silhouette Special Edition® #1334)
Featuring rugged Rafe Antonio, aristocrat by birth,
loner by choice. But not for long....

Coming in November 2000:

A MAN ALONE
(Silhouette Special Edition® #1357)
Featuring Thane Hamilton, a wounded war hero on his way
home to the woman who has always secretly loved him....

*Look for the third book in the series in early 2001! In the
meantime, don't miss Lindsay McKenna's brand-new,
longer-length single title, available in August 2000:*

MORGAN'S MERCENARIES:
HEART OF THE WARRIOR

Only from Lindsay McKenna and
Silhouette Books!

**Intimate Moments is celebrating
Silhouette's 20th Anniversary with
groundbreaking new promotions and star authors:**

Look for these original novels from
New York Times bestselling authors:

In August 2000:
A Game of Chance by **Linda Howard**, #1021

In September 2000:
Night Shield by **Nora Roberts**,
part of NIGHT TALES

Don't miss
A YEAR OF LOVING DANGEROUSLY,
a twelve-book continuity series featuring SPEAR—a
covert intelligence agency. For its equally enigmatic
operatives, love was never part of the mission profile....
Sharon Sala launches the promotion in July 2000
with *Mission: Irresistible*, #1016.

In September 2000, look for the return
of **36 HOURS**, with original stories from
**Susan Mallery, Margaret Watson,
Doreen Roberts** and **Marilyn Pappano.**

And look for:
Who Do You Love?
October 2000, #1033
You won't want to miss this two-in-one collection
featuring **Maggie Shayne** and **Marilyn Pappano!**

Available at your favorite retail outlet.

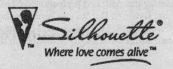

Where love comes alive™

PS20SIM

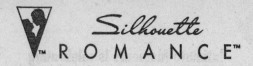

Silhouette ROMANCE™

COMING NEXT MONTH

#1462 THOSE MATCHMAKING BABIES—Marie Ferrarella
Storkville, USA

With the opening of her new day-care center, Hannah Brady was swamped. Then twin babies appeared at the back door! Luckily Dr. Jackson Caldwell was *very* willing to help. In fact, Hannah soon wondered if his interest wasn't more than neighborly....

#1463 CHERISH THE BOSS—Judy Christenberry
The Circle K Sisters

Abby Kennedy was not what Logan Crawford had expected in his new boss. The Circle K's feisty owner was young, intelligent...and beautiful. And though Abby knew a lot about ranching, Logan was hoping *he* could teach *her* a few things—about love!

#1464 FIRST TIME, FOREVER—Cara Colter
Virgin Brides

She was caring for her orphaned nephew. He had a farm to run and a toddler to raise. So Kathleen Miles and Evan Atkins decided on a practical, mutually beneficial union...until the handsome groom decided to claim his virgin bride....

#1465 THE PRINCE'S BRIDE-TO-BE—Valerie Parv
The Carramer Crown

As a favor to her twin sister, Caroline Temple agreed to pose as handsome Prince Michel de Marigny's betrothed. But soon she wanted to be the prince's real-life bride. Yet if he knew the truth, would Michel accept *Caroline* as his wife?

#1466 IN WANT OF A WIFE—Arlene James

Millionaire Channing Hawkins didn't want romance, but he needed a mommy for his daughter. Lovely Jolie Winters was a perfect maternal fit, but Channing soon realized he'd gotten more than he'd wished for...and that love might be part of the package....

#1467 HIS, HERS...OURS?—Natalie Patrick

Her boss was getting married, and perfectionist Shelley Harriman wanted everything flawless. But Wayne Perry, her boss's friend, had entirely different ideas. Could these two get through planning the wedding...and admit there might be another in *their* future?